Christmr

NOELLE ADAMS

I do not at all understand the mystery of grace—only that it meets us where we are but does not leave us where it found us.

Anne Lamott

One

Brie Graves sat in an outdoor café in downtown Savannah and wondered why doing exactly what she wanted for a month had turned out to be so boring.

Two weeks ago, when she'd come to the resolution to spend December having fun, indulging any random whim and not worrying about the future, she'd expected to actually enjoy it. Instead, she'd spent the past twelve days wandering around Savannah, brooding about what she would do after New Year's.

She'd been under contract as a restoration artisan for a variety of church-restoration jobs for the past few years—working primarily with the stained glass, which was her specialty in her historic preservation degree—but her last contract had ended a few weeks ago. She couldn't find any other jobs, even with her skill and experience.

She'd had to give up her lovely apartment and move in with her brother last week, and for all she knew she'd be living there for the foreseeable future. She loved her brother, and they actually got along really well, but he was busy with his career and his wife, and he didn't need a single, jobless sister hanging around all the time.

If no position had opened up as of New Year's, she was going to have to start applying at restaurants and retail stores, which was such a depressing thought she could hardly process it.

Taking a sip of cappuccino, she turned her head to gaze at the small painting she'd been admiring for the past three days.

There was a holiday art festival going on in Savannah this week, and she'd spent hours wandering the stands and exhibits scattered through the historic neighborhood streets. But she kept coming back to this one painting. She loved it so much she would have bought it in an instant, but even five hundred dollars—which was moderately priced for the art at this festival—was far too high for her current budget.

She was about to descend into a full-fledged mope when her phone rang.

She stared down at her brother's name for a full thirty seconds until she finally connected the call. "Hey, Mitchell."

"What are you doing?" he asked rather brusquely. Mitchell had never been known for any particular civility or grace in his manners.

"I'm downtown looking at the art again."

"By yourself?"

"What does it matter?"

"Why don't you hang out with your friends or something?"

She sighed, understanding now the purpose of his call. He might sound rather abrupt, but he was worried about her. "They all have jobs that keep them busy during the days."

"You'll find something else. You always do."

"Contract jobs in historic preservation aren't very easy to come by. I've been lucky these past few years."

"You haven't been lucky. You're good. So you'll find something else."

"We'll see."

"You know you can stay with me for as long as you need. Deanna and I don't care at all."

"I know. I appreciate it." She made sure to sound patient since she really did appreciate her brother and his wife, but she was getting tired of having these conversations. Lately everyone she knew seemed to want to have one with her.

She hated feeling needy that way.

"Deanna thinks you've been avoiding her."

"I haven't been avoiding her!"

"Then why do you spend all day away from the house?"

There was some truth to her sister-in-law's suspicion, but it had nothing to do with not wanting to hang out with Deanna, who was friendly, practical, and kindhearted. It had more to do with the fact that seeing Mitchell and Deanna—who were so happy and satisfied both in career and in their marriage—made Brie feel more like a loser.

"You're not still moping about that bastard Chase, are you?" Mitchell asked, his voice a little rougher, as it always was when he referred to her ex-boyfriend.

"No," Brie said with a sigh. "I'm not."

"You sound mopey to me."

"Well, if you want the truth, I'm not having the best year of my life, but I'm not still hung up on Chase. I know what an ass he was. I don't want anything to do with him anymore. But it's still depressing to know that you were stupid enough to fall for someone like that."

"Everyone falls for the wrong person occasionally."

"You never did."

"Yeah, well, I made my share of mistakes in the romance department. You know that."

Brie did know that. He'd made one mistake after another with Deanna, and she'd called him out on every one of them. She smiled at his self-deprecating tone, feeling a little better despite herself.

"You're laughing at me, aren't you?" Mitchell asked after a pause.

She giggled. "Maybe a little."

"I can live with that. But seriously, Deanna would love to hang out with you. She really loves you. I don't like for you to wander around alone all the time."

"It's not all the time. I'm just taking this month to do exactly what I want, no matter what anyone else thinks. It's kind of a reward for turning thirty soon and for getting over Chase. This is really what I want to do right now. I promise it has nothing to do with Deanna."

"Okay," Mitchell murmured slowly. "As long as it's really what you want."

"It is."

"You're still planning to come up to Eden Manor with us for Christmas though, right?"

Mitchell's sister-in-law, Deanna's sister, owned a bed and breakfast in north Georgia with her husband, and the whole family was planning to get together there for the holidays.

"Yes, of course. I definitely don't want to spend Christmas alone. I'll be there."

"Okay. Good. Things will be fine, you know. You're going to find a new job, and you're better off without Chase."

"I know."

"And it's not the end of the world to turn thirty and live with your brother for a little while."

"I know." She smiled at his tone. "Thanks, Mitchell."

4

He just grunted, which was his normal response to thanks, and she felt encouraged as she disconnected the call.

Her eyes returned instinctively to the painting she loved, but there was a man standing in front of it now so she couldn't see it.

When the man turned his head slightly, she could see his profile and recognized it.

He'd been here yesterday. She'd been sitting in this same spot where she could look at the painting, drink cappuccino, and people-watch without being disturbed, and she'd noticed this man particularly.

She never would have noticed him under normal circumstances. He was middle-aged or a little older, with brown hair with a lot of gray in it, and he wasn't particularly handsome or noteworthy in any way. He had a fit body and upright posture, but he wasn't unusually tall or impressively built. He wore well-tailored tan trousers and a button-up shirt. His features were classically even but with nothing distinctive or eye-catching about his face. He was alone as he'd been the day before.

The only reason she'd noticed him at all was that he'd stood for almost fifteen minutes in front of the painting she loved.

No one else had looked at the painting nearly so long.

She was still watching him when he turned around, and for a moment their eyes met across the sidewalk.

She glanced down in that instinctive way everyone did when they were caught staring at someone else. She fiddled with her phone for a minute, thinking that the man had the most beautiful chocolate-brown eyes she'd ever seen.

He didn't look like a normal tourist. She wondered who he was. She wanted to talk to him, see what he thought about that painting.

5

Then she remembered that she was going to do anything she wanted this month, whether or not it was normal, rational, or expected.

She looked back up and saw he'd come over to the café and was taking a table and asking for a cup of coffee.

As he sat down, he glanced over at her again as if to verify that she was looking at him.

She gave him a little smile, fighting off an automatic wave of self-consciousness. She was usually a friendly, straightforward person, but this man had such a distinguished, set-apart air that it made her a little nervous. "I saw you looking at that painting of the fishing pond," she said.

He nodded, his face relaxing slightly as if he'd suspected she'd been up to no good and now realized she wasn't. "You're not the artist, are you?"

"I wish. No. It's just my favorite."

"It's certainly the best painting in the festival."

"You think so too?" She was strangely pleased to have her perspective confirmed by this man, who came across as both intelligent and incredibly sophisticated, despite his rather ordinary appearance.

"Without doubt." He gave a polite nod to the server who brought him his coffee and then took a slow sip.

This was the moment when the conversation would normally end. They were strangers, after all. One might make a minute's worth of casual conversation with a stranger in a setting like this, but rarely would it last very long.

But Brie was more interested in this man than ever. Not only did he love her painting, but he also didn't speak like anyone she'd ever met.

She was bored, and he was interesting. And she was determined to do anything she wanted this month even if it made her look like a fool.

"I can't figure out what's so good about the painting," she said as if there had been no pause in their conversation. "With the landscape and the rural fishing pond, it should come across as kind of... cheesy, but it doesn't at all. It just... speaks to me."

The man turned his gaze back toward her, and he didn't look annoyed or impatient by the continued conversation. Rather, his eyes rested on her face as if he were genuinely seeing her, genuinely listening to her, taking her seriously. "Art comes across as cheesy when it's calling on feelings but doing so inauthentically. It's doing so only to generate those easy emotions in the viewer without offering anything real to give them meaning. Now those paintings..." He nodded toward another, much more popular exhibit of landscape paintings down the block. "Those are truly cheese." He spoke the last word as if he didn't normally use it, as if he were trying it out.

She chuckled, more stimulated by this conversation than she'd been by anything in weeks. "But everyone loves those. They're going for thousands of dollars, way more than the little fishing pond."

"Naturally. People tend to accept what's easy without considering whether it's real or true. Thus they take in so many half-truths and lies because they make them feel what they want to feel." He shook his head and set down his cup of coffee. "Surely that doesn't surprise you."

"No," she admitted. "It doesn't. I've just never heard it explained that way before. And I love that you just used the word 'thus' as if it were a normal word to use in conversation."

7

The man looked surprised, but then he laughed, and it transformed his face in a way that was almost breathtaking. In that moment, he was incredibly attractive. Brie couldn't look away.

When she realized she was staring rather stupidly, she managed to pull herself together. "You're not from the art school here, are you?"

He arched his eyebrows. "Do I look like I'm from the art school?"

He didn't. At all. He looked like he belonged in some sort of elegant, discreet, high-priced establishment. "Uh, no. Not really. You just seem to know a lot about art."

"They would absolutely hate me at this art school. At *any* art school."

"Why?"

"I'm far too traditional for current tastes. What about you? You're obviously well informed on art." His eyes took her in from her long, loose dark hair to her shoes with beaded insets. She wore a broomstick skirt in a pretty floral print and a rose-colored tunic sweater. She figured she looked too Bohemian for his tastes, and she briefly wished she came across as more sophisticated.

When she processed what she was thinking, she pushed the idea away. She wasn't going to try to morph into a different person for a man. Not any man. Not again. Not after Chase.

She suddenly realized the man was still waiting for an answer. "Oh. I actually did go to the art school, but they didn't much like me either. I was in historic preservation, so it was a different sort of niche. I particularly love churches, and churches are definitely out of style lately with the art crowd."

"Historic preservation? Is that right? Tell me about it."

~

The next day, Brie was sitting at the same table in the same café in view of the same painting.

She'd been sitting there for almost an hour now, and she was starting to feel like an idiot.

The day before, she'd talked to that fascinating man for more than an hour—about art, about historic preservation, about church buildings, and about the jobs in stained glass she'd done over the past few years. She'd never talked to anyone as intelligent, informed, and insightful as he was. He seemed to know something about everything, and he knew a lot about subjects she cared very deeply about.

That conversation was the best thing to happen to her in a really long time, but he'd left with a smile and a polite shake of her hand, without any request for her phone number, without even giving her his name.

So she was back here today, hoping that he'd return too.

She really wanted to see him again, to talk to him, to find out more about him.

It was silly to expect him to come back. He was clearly a mature, successful, cultivated man, quite a bit older than her. He was the most self-contained person she'd ever met. He wasn't likely to be so excited about one random conversation that he'd come back here with the vague hope of seeing her again.

But she was here anyway, getting more disappointed as the minutes passed and he failed to appear.

He probably had a job. He didn't sound like he was from Savannah. His accent had been clean and polished and completely uninflected. He could have been from anywhere in the world. Perhaps he had moved to Georgia from somewhere else, and he'd just been killing time on his lunch break yesterday.

Or he could have been visiting the city and had already flown halfway across the country to his home.

Brie figured she was pretty enough, with dark hair and a slim figure, but she wasn't anything special. She was at least twenty years younger than the man, and she probably hadn't made any sort of real impression on him.

He wasn't going to show up here again today. Waiting for him was silly.

It made her feel weak and needy, which she'd been feeling far too often lately.

Suddenly a wave of embarrassment washed over her. She didn't want to be the kind of person who would wait with bated breath for a particular man to stroll by, when the man had offered her no reason to expect it.

She wasn't going to be this person.

And she would never admit to anyone that she'd done this.

She left a tip on her table and slid her book into her bag, standing up and ducking her head as she mentally pulled herself together, giving up the faint fantasy of getting to know that man.

She was starting to walk away when a voice came from beside her. "Are you leaving?"

She sucked in a breath and turned to see the man from yesterday, watching her with slightly raised eyebrows.

"Oh. Uh, yeah. I guess so."

"That's too bad." He gave her a little smile. "I enjoyed our talk yesterday."

Her self-consciousness transformed into pleasure and excitement at the knowledge that she hadn't been completely stupid after all.

The conversation had been something special. He'd thought so too. It wasn't just in her imagination. She hadn't blown it all out of proportion because she was a little bit needy right now. "I did too," she admitted, her cheeks flushing slightly.

She waited a moment to see if he'd say anything else, if he'd invite her to lunch, to dinner, to something.

When he didn't, she remembered that this was the month she was going to do anything she wanted, whether or not it was scary.

She wasn't a particularly shy person. She'd even asked men out before. But only after they'd made it clear they were interested in her. So it was definitely a little scary, but she heard herself saying, "Did you want to have lunch with me?"

His eyes widened slightly, and he didn't respond immediately.

She ducked her head, letting her hair slide down to cover her face slightly. "I'm sorry," she said in a rush. "I didn't mean to make it weird or awkward. I know we don't know each other. I don't even know your name. You might be married for all I know, or not interested in... Anyway, I really did enjoy talking to you yesterday."

The man's expression changed, as if he'd come to some sort of resolution within himself. "I'm not married. I would love to have lunch with you. And my name is Cyrus."

~

They went to lunch at a small, charming French restaurant Cyrus had discovered last week, and he kept telling himself not to be a fool.

He'd already been rather foolish, he had to admit.

He'd seen Brie for the first time two days ago, sitting by herself in the café, gazing soulfully at the painting of the fishing pond. She'd caught his attention immediately, not only because she was so delicately pretty, but also because she was so clearly taken by the one painting that made the entire festival worth his visit.

She hadn't noticed him, but Cyrus was used to that. Unless people knew he was *the* Cyrus Damon—business mogul and eccentric billionaire—they tended to overlook him.

So yesterday he'd ended up back by the painting, partly to see it again but partly because he wanted to see her again.

Just see her. She was far too young for him—probably younger than his nephews—even if Cyrus had any romantic dreams left in his soul.

He didn't.

Some people just weren't created for romance. He was one of those people.

He'd still felt his heart do a little jump when he'd spotted her at the same table and then again when she'd smiled at him.

He'd been in Savannah for eleven days, and that conversation with Brie was the only thing that had genuinely engaged him in all that time.

But he'd spent his life being wise and careful, which was why he'd tried very hard not to come back to the same corner today. In fact, he'd made a point of not doing so, and it was so strange and inexplicable that he'd ended up here anyway.

He couldn't believe she'd asked him to lunch. He couldn't believe she wanted to spend time with him. She was so much younger than him, and women were only ever interested in him for his money.

Brie didn't know who he was. She had no idea he was Cyrus Damon. He'd gotten very good at recognizing the telltale signs of mercenary women, and he knew for sure she wasn't one of them. Which meant it was *him* she wanted to spend time with.

He kept telling himself he had nothing else to do this month—since his family had forced this extended vacation on him—so he might as well enjoy himself. He wouldn't do anything stupid, and he wouldn't have unrealistic expectations about it turning into more than a lunch.

What could be the harm, after all?

So they went to the French restaurant he suggested, and they talked more about art, and about the history of Savannah, and about the food, and about various places that they'd traveled. She seemed completely wrapped up in the conversation, as if it was as interesting to her as it was to him, and she kept smiling at him as if she liked what she saw.

It was so strange. So unusual for him. For a beautiful young woman to gaze at him like that.

Women threw themselves at Cyrus all the time, for his name or his money or his power. He could always recognize it, and he found it decidedly distasteful.

There was nothing like that in Brie's manner. No guile or artifice of any kind.

The whole thing was… intoxicating.

He didn't want to be a dirty old man though. He'd never been that sort of person. So when his mind started to travel down certain exciting avenues, he rigorously controlled it.

That simply wasn't who he was, no matter how lovely and mesmerizing Brie happened to be to him at the moment.

They were eating dessert when his phone vibrated for the third time. He'd ignored it previously, but he was starting to worry that something seriously was wrong. So he pulled it out and glanced down to see the caller was his nephew, Benjamin.

"I'm so sorry," he murmured to Brie. "He's called three times now, and I'm afraid something might be wrong. Do you mind?"

"Of course not," she said. "Please take it."

When he answered the phone, Benjamin demanded, "Where are you? Is everything all right?"

His youngest nephew had warmed up quite a bit in the past few years, after falling in love and getting married, but he still tended toward the blunt and gruff, so his tone didn't particularly trouble Cyrus. "Of course it is. What do you mean?"

"You were supposed to come over to Mom's for lunch."

Cyrus blinked. "I wasn't aware of any plans."

"She said she mentioned it, and you said you'd try to make it."

"Oh, I'm sorry. I completely forgot, and I hadn't realized it was a firm commitment. Please apologize to her."

"You better do it yourself."

"I will."

"You're not working, are you?"

"No. I'm not working." He narrowed his eyes. All four of his nephews had been pestering him for the past two weeks, making sure he was following their plan of giving up work for the entire month of December, which was one of the hardest things Cyrus had ever done.

"Then what are you doing?"

"I'm having lunch."

"Alone?"

"No."

There was a pause, as Ben took this in. "Who are you with?"

"I didn't realize I needed to report all my comings and goings to you," Cyrus said coolly.

Ben gave a huff that might have been amusement. "Right. Sorry. Okay. Have fun. Call up Mom later and apologize."

"I will."

Cyrus was shaking his head as he disconnected the call.

"Were you supposed to be somewhere else?" Brie asked, raising her eyes from her plate to his face.

"No. It was a misunderstanding."

"You can leave if you need to."

"I don't need to. I don't want to. I'll visit my sister this afternoon. It will be fine."

"So she lives in town?"

"Yes. That's why I'm vacationing here. My family got together and had a kind of intervention for me because they believe I work too hard. They insisted I take a month off, and they arranged for me to come here so I could spend time with my sister."

Brie's eyes widened. "Did you really need an intervention?"

"I don't believe so. I do work a lot, but I don't think it's unhealthy. But I also don't want everyone to worry about me, so I agreed to their... plan."

"Are you staying with your sister then?"

"No. I took a house. We both prefer to have our space."

"I can definitely understand that. I'm living with my brother right now. He and his wife are great, but I can't wait to have a place of my own again."

He opened his mouth to ask a question but then closed it again. He was curious about why she was staying with her brother, about why she couldn't live on her own at present, but it might be pushy or intrusive to ask on such short acquaintance.

"My work is all contract labor," she explained as if she'd read his mind. "My last contract ended a few weeks ago, and I haven't found anything else yet. My particular skill set has limited opportunities, and my apartment was expensive. Really it was too expensive for my income, even before. But it was so beautiful—in a converted Victorian. I loved it so much, and I just had to have it."

Even on such short acquaintance, he could see why she would take an apartment she loved even if it was beyond her budget. She was clearly passionate and spontaneous and a lover of beauty.

Like him.

Like him in being a lover of beauty. He'd never been spontaneous in his life.

It was a real shame that the work she did was in such low demand. It was needed in the world—restoring the beautiful things of the past rather than throwing up more sterile, cookie-cutter structures.

Instead of saying that, he asked, "Are you looking beyond Savannah for work?"

"I'm going to have to, I think, if I want to keep doing what I'm doing. There's actually a lot of potential here in Savannah—with all the historic buildings—but that doesn't mean I'll always be able to find something." She sighed and leaned back in her seat. "What I really need is a city with a lot of crumbling churches."

He chuckled. "I wonder if there's research out there on the number of crumbling churches per capita."

He actually reached for his phone to call Melissa Forester, who handled all that kind of research for him. She'd be able to find an answer for them in no time at all. But he didn't complete the motion.

Brie would start to get curious if he showed her he had resources like that.

He didn't want her to get curious about his identity.

He wanted to simply enjoy her company for the time being since obviously it would never go any further.

He cleared his throat and was completely shocked when he heard himself asking, "So do you have plans for tomorrow?"

Her eyes widened again in that particular look she had—as if he'd surprised and pleased her at the same time. The expression caused his chest to clench in a way he could hardly remember happening to him before.

"No." She gave him a rueful smile. "I don't have any plans at all until Christmas. I'm just... drifting."

"I am too," he admitted.

"Well, maybe we could keep each other company." She looked momentarily self-conscious, as if she was a little embarrassed by her suggestion. The look was lovely, charming, irresistible.

What was wrong with him, that he was so wrapped up in one small expression from this woman?

"I would enjoy that," Cyrus admitted. "I'm just wondering if it's wise. I'm only going to be in town for another week or so."

"I understand that. I've got my own life too. I would never expect... anything... but your company. We both have our own lives, and hanging out would have nothing to do with the rest of our lives. But I've been... I don't know... kind of lost lately, and I've had such a good time with you. I completely understand if you'd rather do something else."

She was trying so hard to explain her expectations without presuming too much, and he understood her completely.

She wasn't looking for a relationship—not from him. They just matched each other in an utterly unpredictable way, so it would be a shame not to enjoy it for a little while longer.

"I've had a good time with you too," he said at last. "And I think we're in the same situation in terms of... lostness right now." He smiled at her, his heart skipping in excitement despite his attempt to mentally talk some sense into it.

"So when are you planning to leave Savannah?" she asked.

"On Monday." He and his nephew Harrison's family were going to a bed and breakfast in north Georgia for some relaxing time before Christmas.

"Okay. So maybe we agree to just spend this week together—until Sunday. No expectations beyond that, no personal questions, no last names even. Just Brie and Cyrus—for this one week. What about that?"

He'd almost swear she looked excited at the thought—as if that kind of week with him was exactly what she wanted.

It would be foolish. No question. But he had to admit it was what he wanted too. "I agree to those terms," he said after just a moment.

Her smile warmed even more.

Feeling happy in a way that wasn't at all like him, he added, "I need to have dinner with my sister and nephew this evening, but may I show you a few of my favorite churches in Savannah tomorrow?"

The smile on her face, like the sun breaking out from the clouds, caused him to momentarily lose his breath. "I would love that."

Cyrus Damon tried to remember the last time anyone had been so genuinely pleased to spend time with him—just time, no strategies or expectations.

And he honestly couldn't remember if anyone ever had.

Two

"So who is this guy?" Deanna asked, splashing some cream in her coffee and coming over to sit across the kitchen table from Brie.

"I told you. He's just a guy I met. It's nothing important." Brie didn't know why she was so embarrassed. She'd gone out with plenty of men and had never had trouble talking about them. But this felt different, private.

"But who is he?" Deanna was lovely, small with thick dark hair and big eyes of an unusual pale green. She was smiling irrepressibly, despite the fact that it was just six thirty in the morning.

"Wait, there's a guy? What guy?" Mitchell had just walked in, fully dressed in a suit for work. He owned a hotel in town—and had recently acquired a restaurant as well—and he always worked very hard.

"There's not a guy!" Brie exclaimed.

"There *is* a guy," Deanna said, her mouth twitching in amusement. "She's going to spend the day with him."

"Who is he?" Mitchell got his coffee and sat down too.

Brie was flushed and frustrated although it was perfectly natural that they'd be curious and interested. They both cared about her. They would be excited if she was.

She just didn't know what to tell them about Cyrus.

"I just met him the other day," she explained. "We talked about art and architecture and things like that. He's going to show me some of his favorite churches today. It's really nothing. He's on vacation by himself, so we're both just… killing time."

"So there's no potential for more?" Deanna asked.

Brie gave a half shrug. "I don't think so. He's a lot older than me, and he seems… He's obviously not looking for romance. We just have a lot in common and have a good time together. Please don't get all excited about it."

"Okay," Mitchell said. "Fair enough." Then he frowned. "How much older?"

Brie almost groaned. "I don't know. He's like… middle-aged." That was vague enough and could count for the ages of forty to sixty. She didn't know how old Cyrus was, but it was surely somewhere in that range. She was sure he wasn't yet at retirement age.

"That doesn't sound too bad," Deanna said. "Mitchell is eight years older than me, and James is more than nine years older than Rose. This guy sounds doable to me."

"Let's not talk about my little sister *doing* some old guy," Mitchell grumbled.

Torn between amusement and embarrassment, Brie replied, "Would you all stop! I'm not *doing* anyone! We're just talking about art and stuff. He might be gay for all I know."

Cyrus wasn't gay. She was absolutely sure of it. But she wasn't going to share this conviction with her brother and sister-in-law.

She was really excited about today, but she wasn't going to tell them that either.

~

Cyrus glanced at the gilt-framed mirror in the entryway of his rented house, wondering if there was something else he should do about his appearance.

He looked as he always looked—which had never been particularly impressive, even when he was younger. It was silly to expect a miracle transformation now. Brie wasn't going to be blown away by his appearance. The thought shouldn't have even crossed his mind.

He'd always been cerebral, intentional, completely in control of his actions. He was capable of spending time with Brie without getting his hopes up about anything else.

"Do you need anything, sir?"

The quiet, eminently civilized voice broke through Cyrus's reverie. He looked over his shoulder at Gordon, who had been his butler and manservant for decades. "No, thank you, Gordon."

"We have fresh flowers in the vases here. I could arrange some in a bouquet for the young lady if you'd like."

Cyrus's eyebrows shot up. "I'm not going to bring her flowers."

"I see, sir."

Gordon was never anything less than completely professional, but he could still make his opinions more than clear. He looked vaguely disapproving now, as if Cyrus should have been making more of a romantic effort with Brie.

"This isn't a date," Cyrus said.

"I understand."

"We are just… spending the day together."

"Of course, sir."

"She doesn't want romance from me. She's far too young. It would be completely inappropriate."

"I agree, sir."

Cyrus shot Gordon a quick look, immediately defensive of the other man's agreement, when the sentiment was one he was trying to convince himself about.

Gordon's expression was utterly bland. "So no flowers, sir?"

"No flowers."

"I would be happy to prepare dinner for you both tonight if you'd like to bring her back to the house."

Cyrus's whole body gave a completely ridiculous clench of excitement at this suggestion. He prayed Gordon hadn't been able to see his response. "I will not be bringing her back here."

"As you wish, sir."

Cyrus shook his head. What he wished for was never going to happen.

~

"This is the strangest church I've ever seen," Brie said a few hours later, staring up at the vaulted ceiling of the small nave.

Cyrus had taken her to a few different churches so far in Savannah, and they'd both had a great time discussing the art and architecture. But this small, out-of-the-way church was his favorite in the city—and in fact one of his favorites in the world. So, despite himself, he was a little disappointed by her first comment on it. "It is rather unusual," he admitted.

"It's got multiple personalities," she said, bringing her eyes down to his face. "This part looks pretty traditional, but that narthex was totally different."

"The church was built in different stages over hundreds of years. So it reflects styles from multiple eras."

Brie just kept staring around as if she couldn't quite get a handle on it.

They walked around, Cyrus pointing out some highlights and explaining some of the history, doing his best not to defend the appeal of the building. He tried to read her expression as she gazed around at unusual stained glass and varied architecture.

He'd found this church almost twenty years ago on one of his visits to his sister. It was on the register of historic places, but it wasn't one of the normal tourist spots. It still housed a dying Episcopal congregation, but the building was open to the public during the days—for the few visitors who wanted to admire the strange structures and decorations.

Cyrus was normally inclined toward classic symmetry—in architecture and in life—so he wasn't sure why this old place held such an appeal for him.

But he loved this church, and he was hoping Brie would at least like it.

When she asked about the oldest part of the church, he led her to the chancel.

"Wow," Brie murmured.

"The chancel is from the original church, which burned down not long after it was built," Cyrus said, hoping her response meant she was starting to change her impressions. "You can see the line of demarcation here where they started building the new church around it."

Brie stared and stared, and peered and peered, and circled around without saying a word. And the longer the silence stretched on, the more absurdly nervous Cyrus became. It didn't really matter, he told himself, whether she liked this place or not.

"You know," she said finally, lowering her eyes from the round stained glass window over the cross. "This is my kind of God."

Cyrus blinked. "What?"

Brie looked a little embarrassed, as if that wasn't exactly what she'd intended to say. "I mean, the kind of God who is... is evoked in a church like this is closer to how I'd imagine him." She swallowed and gave him a frustrated look. "Don't look at me like I'm crazy. I'm just not saying it very well."

"I don't think you're crazy," Cyrus said, his voice reflecting some of his relief, despite his attempt to sound normal. "But maybe explain a little more."

"I mean at old cathedrals and most of the grand historic churches in the States—those with pure Gothic or neo-Gothic architecture—we're supposed to envision God as vast, awe-inspiring, miles and miles above us. And I suppose, theologically, that's the point. We see some of that here—we get some of the Gothic uplift in the main sanctuary. But... but all the different architectural styles kind of temper it. We see evidence of all kinds of people, with hundreds of years in between, trying to worship God in their own way. It's not pure. It's... it's real. And I was just thinking that this is the kind of God who might love someone as quirky and messed up as me." She looked down at the floor as if she'd embarrassed herself. "I suppose that sounds silly."

Cyrus experienced a wave of enlightenment, of understanding, of bonding. Her ramblings were a far deeper tribute to his beloved church than any traditional compliment or empty praise. He realized she loved it too.

He reached out to softly touch her arm. "It doesn't sound silly."

She gave him a smile that was almost shy.

"So are you religious?" Cyrus said before he could think through whether such a comment was wise or strategic. They weren't supposed to be asking each other personal questions.

Her eyes flickered over to his face but didn't rest there. "I'm not. At least not in any traditional way. My family never went to church or anything. But I believe in some things."

"What do you believe in?" To his surprise, Cyrus really wanted to know.

She shifted self-consciously. "You'll laugh."

Cyrus shook his head. They both seemed to have entered the hushed mood of the place, and there was no room for irony here. "I won't laugh."

Brie studied his face for a long moment. Then she turned around to stare at the simple cross above the altar, glinting with the shifting light of the sanctuary. It took her a long time to answer. Then finally she said, very softly, "I believe in love and... and sacrifice—and especially when they exist together. I think it's called... I think it's called grace. I believe that's the most important thing. I believe that's what makes the world beautiful."

In a different context, the words might have sounded either pretentious or overly sentimental. But Cyrus had no desire to laugh or cringe. He followed her gaze to the gilded Christ on the cross, the ultimate symbol of love and sacrifice for so many people, in so many places, over so many centuries of time.

For no particular reason, he thought without warning about his nephew Harrison, who'd quietly shown him unfaltering love and loyalty for so long, even when Cyrus had done nothing to deserve it.

He was moved in a completely unexpected way, and it took him a moment to recover.

She darted him a nervous little look. "I know it sounds vague and too abstract to be a real belief system. And I don't know how it works out on the... on the cosmic level. But that's what I believe in."

Cyrus knew her then—in a more intimate way than he'd ever have expected to know someone whose life had just briefly brushed up against his. He understood a truth about her. A truth that exposed her, made her vulnerable.

It was a gift she had given him, and it meant something to him. "I understand," he breathed.

They stood in silence for a long time.

Then finally Brie turned back toward him. "What do you believe in?" She almost whispered the words as if she weren't sure how he would respond.

Cyrus instinctively looked upward, at the architecture designed to raise the human spirit toward heaven. He swallowed, and he told Brie the truth. "I believe in power."

The nature of her silence prompted him to check her expression, and he blinked when he saw she looked disappointed.

Afraid she hadn't understood, that she thought he was belittling her confession earlier and ignoring the mood they had shaped, he hurried on, "I don't mean political or social machinations. I mean I believe that real power exists in the universe and it doesn't rest in us."

Her face changed. Like she understood.

Something relaxed in his chest and let him to continue, "That's why we live our lives trying to cling to whatever little bits of power we have, why we're always grappling for order and justice. But we have no real control—not over anything but our immediate actions."

He thought about how he'd lived so many years of his life, holding on to the few threads of life he could control. "That's why power has always been at the root of human experience. It exists—somewhere. But it isn't ours."

He let out a long breath, experiencing the oddest sensation. That he'd been understood on the deepest level, in a way he could never remember before.

But then he realized what he'd revealed about himself. He stiffened, had to fight not to pull away from Brie, who was standing quietly beside him.

What was he thinking, opening up so deeply to a stranger? He never opened up to anyone—not even his family.

He felt like he'd been stripped naked.

But Brie seemed to know how to respond to the moment. She gave him a little smile. "Thank you for telling me that. You know what I want?"

He managed to arch an eyebrow in a quizzical look and not drop his eyes.

"I need coffee. Shall we find a café?"

Cyrus could have slumped over in relief at the change of subject, the return to reality, the shedding of whatever bizarre spell had come over him in this place. "Sounds like an excellent plan to me."

~

Three hours later, it was midafternoon, and Cyrus was trying to convince himself that his day with Brie should really be coming to an end.

He'd already spent more time with her than was good for him. All day, he'd felt excited, stimulated, deeply involved.

Almost young.

And now he was thinking far too much about how beautiful Brie was, how sensual her laughter was, how graceful and alluring the line of her neck, the fall of her hair, the curve of her hips.

That line of thinking would just lead him into trouble, but he couldn't seem to rein in his mind—or his eyes. He was letting his eyes linger again on her face and body as they sat on a bench in one of the squares off Bull Street, and the bright sunshine was gilding her brown hair and clear skin a beautiful gold.

He kept reminding himself that the person he'd been today—spending time with a beautiful, intelligent, sincere, passionate, young woman without a thought for the appropriateness of such behavior at his age and position—wasn't who he really was.

He was Cyrus Damon. He would have to go back to being that man very soon.

Brie smiled vividly at him just then, causing his heart to do a ridiculous little skip.

Maybe he didn't have to go back to being that man quite yet.

"Are you having dinner with your sister and nephew again tonight?" she asked.

"No. Not tonight." Cyrus remembered Gordon's suggestion earlier, about her having dinner with him at the house. It wasn't something he should even consider. It was completely out of bounds. It would be wrong in every way. "You could come over to my house this evening for dinner if you'd like," he heard himself saying.

Brie's cheeks flushed a deeper pink, and she slanted him another shy look. "I would like that. Thank you. Will you be cooking?"

Cyrus wasn't at all sure how it had happened, but he was evidently having dinner with Brie after all. "Not me. But I can promise the food will be excellent."

~

Brie couldn't remember ever having such a good day.

It wasn't just that she found Cyrus attractive—although she did, more and more, in a way she never would have expected. But it was like *all* of herself was engaged in being with him—her intellect, her creativity, her emotions, her physical body.

She felt *whole* with him in a way she never had with Chase—or with any other man, for that matter. The age difference between them didn't seem to matter at all. They were just themselves, and they... matched.

So, by evening, she was pulsing with excitement, wondering what might happen after dinner. She knew better than to expect anything that occurred between them to lead to a future. Both of them understood this was just for a week, but that didn't mean they couldn't go further than talking.

She wanted to go further than talking.

She wanted to—a lot.

They parted ways to rest for a while before dinner, so she headed back to Mitchell's house, relieved to find it empty. She wasn't in the mood to try to explain her plans to her brother and sister-in-law, or why she was so excited about it. She looked through her clothes, spending far more time than she should have trying to decide what to wear.

She once more had the fleeting wish that she looked more elegant and sexy, more sophisticated. Cyrus was the kind of man who would probably gravitate toward those kinds of women. Not a woman with a casual, artsy style made up primarily of long skirts and tunic tops made in pretty, unusual prints.

But she made herself brush the thought aside. Over and over again she'd put aside her true nature to make Chase happy, and she'd just ended up miserable. She wasn't going to do it again—even for Cyrus.

She ended up choosing a soft, flowing cotton dress that was flattering but didn't look like she was trying too hard. She also picked out pretty underwear and took a long shower before she dressed.

Cyrus had given her directions, and she arrived at exactly seven o'clock. The house was in one of the historic neighborhoods, and it was beautiful in the Italianate style and very large, with a stone wall around the yard and a doorbell that chimed very loudly.

A man answered the door she didn't recognize.

"Oh," she said, feeling a chill of self-consciousness. "I'm sorry. Maybe I'm in the wrong place. I was looking for Cyrus." She felt rather silly, not even knowing his last name.

"You're in the right place, miss," the man said. "Please come in."

She blinked at the man, wondering who he was. "I'm Brie."

"I know you are, miss. I'm Gordon. I'm on staff with Mr.... Cyrus."

She caught the slight stumble over the name, and she wondered if he'd been instructed about keeping the situation first name only.

She didn't mind. That was one of the terms she and Cyrus had agreed to.

"It's nice to meet you, Gordon. So you, uh, work for Cyrus?"

"Yes, I do."

"Are you a butler?" she asked, grinning at the possibility. She'd never thought to meet a real, live butler before.

Gordon chuckled and gestured down the hall. "Among other things. Mr. Cyrus is waiting for you in the garden since it's such a mild evening."

Brie walked through the house, which was beautifully decorated with high-end antiques, and then exited through French doors onto a paved patio. She gasped at the sight of the landscaped yard, complete with trees, shrubbery, potted winter plants, a small fountain, and even an in-ground hot tub in a far corner.

Cyrus had changed clothes too and was now wearing trousers and a black shirt. He smiled at her and looked so unexpectedly attractive and appealing that Brie felt her heart flutter with anxiety.

She was determined to do exactly as she wanted this month, but she needed to keep control of her emotions enough to not lead herself into needless heartache.

She had a tendency to jump into things headfirst. She got a degree in a field with very few job prospects. She gave herself over to relationships with men who weren't good for her. She'd rented an apartment she couldn't really afford.

She was almost thirty now. Eventually she would have to be smarter. And she could already tell that her emotions were in danger with Cyrus, who was the epitome of an unavailable man.

"This house is absolutely beautiful," she said, searching for normal conversation.

"I do like it," Cyrus murmured, his eyes running up and down her body as if he appreciated what he saw. "And speaking of beautiful, you look absolutely lovely."

She felt herself blushing. She wasn't sure how he did it, but he made simple compliments like that mean more than they should. He made her feel more special with a few words than Chase did when he was actually having sex with her. "Thank you. Surely this house isn't a normal vacation rental."

"No. It's not. I know the owner, and he was kind enough to lend it to me."

"It's absolutely amazing. This garden is…" She trailed off, unsure of how to even describe it.

"Let me show you around."

They walked around the beautifully designed garden for a few minutes, and she went into a minor fit of ecstasy over a sculpture hidden away in one corner, which was one of the most charming things she'd ever seen. When they returned from their stroll, Brie found that Gordon had set up an intimate table near the fountain—complete with candles, white table cloth, crystal stemware, delicate china, and a tall bud vase holding two perfect white lilies.

Brie's lips parted at the beautiful table, and she turned to Cyrus with a question in her eyes.

His lips quirked slightly. "Gordon suggested dinner in the gardens. Who was I to say no?"

Brie couldn't help but laugh although the scene was so romantic that her heart fluttered even more. She let Cyrus help her into her seat and then was well on her way to being swept away as Gordon brought out course after course of mouth-watering, gourmet food and fine, local wine.

By the time they got to the chocolate mousse—served in delicate crystal—Brie was pretty sure she wouldn't have the will to say no to a pickpocket. Cyrus had been charming and charismatic, chatting about Brie's work and later about the history of the churches they'd visited earlier. And his face in the moonlight and candlelight was strangely mesmerizing. Not classically handsome but with so much experience and character in the lines and contours, highlighted by those beautiful chocolate-brown eyes, that she couldn't tear her eyes away.

When they'd finished the last of the wine and the mousse had been licked clean, Brie put down her spoon and collapsed back in her chair. "Wow. That was probably the best dinner—the best meal—I've ever had."

Cyrus smiled at her, almost fondly. "Good. I'll tell Gordon you appreciated it."

"Who decided on the menu and... ambience?"

He arched his eyebrows in amused irony. "It was Gordon. He was very pleased about this dinner, and he might have gone a bit too far in setting the mood."

Intrigued, Brie felt a little less boneless, so she managed to lean forward, resting her head on one hand. "Really? Does he do a lot of matchmaking for you?"

"He never has before," Cyrus said with a half shrug. "I was as surprised as you were."

"Were you really? You acted totally suave, like you have romantic dinners like this all the time."

"I doubt you'd believe me if I told you how long it's been since I've had a romantic meal of any kind."

A surge of curiosity banished a lot of her decadent languor. "How long?" she demanded.

Cyrus's mouth twisted into what might have been a sheepish smile. "I don't think I'm going to tell you."

"But I want to know."

His eyes transformed as he gazed at her. The shift was almost imperceptible, but Brie felt a shudder shape itself in the base of her spine in response to his expression. "Do you always get what you want?" Cyrus asked, his voice throaty, the texture making her shudder even more.

"No," she admitted. "Almost never."

"There's something wrong with a world where such a thing is true."

It took her a minute to unravel this comment, but when she did she was moved even more. The man didn't even seem to be trying, but he had the knack for always saying the right thing, for being kind and romantic and civilized, all at exactly the same time.

She'd never believed it was possible before.

She knew she was treading in dangerous waters here. She was on the verge of being swept away by him completely. She wanted to enjoy herself with him this week, but she didn't want to do something so foolish it would leave her hurt and lonely next week.

She didn't know this man. Not really. So she could feel a resistance rising inside her, at the same time as the deep attraction.

She needed to change the mood between them. Quickly.

"Let's walk some more," she suggested lightly. "I could use it after such a meal."

He stood up and took her hand to help her out of her seat. Then he didn't let her hand go as they strolled through the gardens again.

She soon realized her suggestion might have been a mistake. The rich scent of the air, the soft moonlight, and the feel of Cyrus's warm hand quickly went to her head. She felt unsteady, overly warm, and so fluttery she couldn't take a deep breath.

"God, Cyrus!" she gasped, as an ache of need pulsed through her before she was ready to handle it.

Cyrus had appeared calm, leisurely, at his ease. But he'd evidently been fighting feelings of his own. Her breathless cry seemed to snap his control. He used his clasp on her hand to pivot her around and then slid his free arm around her, pressing her against the length of his body.

His warm, lean strength was exactly what Brie wanted to feel. She freed her hand from his and instinctively twined her arms around his neck. With his hand now free, he used it to cup the back of her head.

"You're so beautiful, Brie," he murmured thickly. "So beautiful and... and glowing with life." His eyes like flames, almost fierce in the moonlight, he leaned his head down to claim her lips.

She responded immediately, opening eagerly to the questioning advance of his tongue and rubbing her breasts against his firm chest.

He made a rough sound in his throat as he moved his mouth urgently against hers and tangled his tongue with hers. One of his hands was still curved around her skull, holding her head steady for his kiss. But the other one was stroking up and down her back.

Arousal pulsing between her legs, Brie clutched at Cyrus's neck and shoulders. Irresistibly drawn as the kiss grew deeper, one of her hands slid up to his hair. Her fingers tangled into it, and the little guttural sounds he made in response were the sexiest things she'd ever heard.

He finally broke off the kiss but only to bury his face against her neck, nuzzling the delicate skin of her throat. She moaned helplessly and arched back. She would have fallen had Cyrus's arms not held her stable.

"Cyrus," she gasped, pressing his head against her neck when he found the tender spot at her pulse.

He grunted in response, mouthing and flicking his tongue on her skin.

She tried to cling to the threads of her control, but her body knew what it wanted, knew it wanted Cyrus. "Cyrus," she gasped again when she felt his hand much lower on her back.

Then suddenly he released her, panting heavily as he gazed across the few inches between them. "I... I didn't intend to do that," he said at last, his voice much rougher than it normally was. "Are you all right, Brie?"

She was flushed and panting and brutally disappointed at the end of the embrace.

And also a little relieved.

This was happening so fast—it was intoxicating and terrifying both. She'd never known a man who'd pulled out of an embrace that had gone so far, and it just made her appreciate Cyrus even more.

"Yes," she said breathlessly. "Of course. It was... a really good kiss."

"Yes. Yes, it was. But I should never have let it go so far."

"It was fine," she said, finally catching her breath. "Really. I... wanted to."

His eyes were searching her face now almost urgently. "I'm far too old for you, Brie."

"But that doesn't really matter, does it? Not if we're only going to spend the week together. Age doesn't make a difference in such a situation."

"Doesn't it?"

"I don't think so. It's not about a future together or anything like that. It's just about... right now."

"Even so, I'm not in the habit of losing control like that."

"We both got a little swept away." She gave him a little smile, wanting to make him relax again, wanting to make him feel better. "Must be the moonlight."

She let out a breath when she saw an ironic twitch of his lips. "Or maybe Gordon put something in the mousse."

She laughed, but it caught in her throat when he reached out to take her hand in both of his. "Brie," he murmured thickly. "Tell me the truth. Do you think less of me now?"

"No!" She was so surprised she stared at him. "No, of course not." She dropped her eyes as she admitted, "To tell you the truth, I like you even more."

"And you still want to spend the week with me?"

"Yes. Definitely." Her eyes flew back up to his face. "Don't you?"

"Yes. I do."

She smiled, feeling warm and happy and rather swoony again. "Okay then. Very good. Then we're fine. You'll have to let me pick our activities tomorrow then."

"That sounds like an excellent plan. Now I'd better get you to your car before I'm less than a gentleman again. You're far too beautiful in the moonlight."

He escorted her back to her car and even offered to drive her home so she wouldn't have to do it herself. She refused, of course, but she found it a sweet gesture.

He kissed her very gently before he said goodnight, and she just about melted into her car seat.

She was thinking as she drove away that she'd never really known a gentleman before. The guys she'd dated had been anything but.

It was different, being treated like she was genuinely special, like she was worthy of extra effort.

She liked it. A lot. Even though it meant she was driving home without having all her physical urges satisfied.

She couldn't help but wonder how a man like Cyrus—so thoughtful and intelligent and attractive and romantic—was still unattached.

A woman with any sense should have snatched him up a long time ago.

Three

Cyrus was drinking coffee and scanning through e-mail on his tablet at just after seven the following morning.

After his intense feelings and responses the evening before, he hadn't expected to sleep very well. But he had. For over six hours, which was more than he normally slept. This morning he felt relaxed and strangely invigorated, excited about seeing Brie again.

It had been far more difficult than it should have been to pull back from her the night before—to not give into the intensity of his desire, which had astonished him with its power and with how quickly it had risen inside him. He was a normal, healthy man, of course, but at his age he wasn't used to such intense physical responses. He was glad he'd controlled himself though.

Brie deserved more than to be an outlet for his long-repressed physical needs.

Pushing the thought away, he tried to focus on his tablet. His assistants were taking care of his e-mail this month, so his in-box wasn't as unmanageable as he would have otherwise expected, and he couldn't summon the energy to worry about the e-mails that were still there, waiting for him to get to after the holidays.

It had been years since anything had shifted his focus from work for long.

A great number of years.

"You're not checking your e-mail, are you?" a familiar male voice came from behind him.

Cyrus turned to see Harrison, his oldest nephew, approaching with a smile. "Harrison! What are you doing here, son?" He stood up to return the brief hug Harrison gave him.

"You didn't answer my question."

"You realize the appalling irony of chastising anyone else for checking e-mail on vacation, don't you?" Cyrus smiled as he took his seat again, gesturing Harrison into the chair beside him. "Is Gordon getting you breakfast?"

"Thank you. Yes." Harrison's mouth twitched up. "To both the breakfast and the irony. But I told you we were taking care of everything important while you're on a break. You really don't have to worry."

"I'm not worrying." A couple of weeks ago, Cyrus never would have believed he could leave his work behind for so long and not worry about what was happening in his absence, but it was true. For the past few days, he hadn't worried about his work at all.

At all.

"Good." Harrison smiled at Gordon, who'd brought him out a plate of eggs, bacon, and croissant, as well as a cup of coffee. "Thank you, Gordon."

"You're welcome, sir." Gordon took Cyrus's nearly empty cup to refill it.

"So why are you here then?" Cyrus asked, returning his focus to his nephew. "I thought you were spending the week in Atlanta, preparing for the launch of the new tearoom. Aren't Marietta and Melissa with you?"

"They are. They're still in Atlanta. I'm just here for a quick stop. Ben called me."

Cyrus suddenly realized why his nephew had made the completely unexpected trip to Savannah. He arched his eyebrows coolly. "He's worried?"

"He is. So is Aunt Lucy. They think you're not acting like yourself at all. You disappear for hours every day. You missed a lunch. You won't answer their questions about what you've been doing. You're acting... distracted. They're worried." Harrison looked slightly uncomfortable. He'd never liked to have these kinds of conversations.

Cyrus didn't like them either. "There is nothing to worry about."

"So then what's going on with you?"

Clearing his throat, Cyrus wondered how he should answer the question. He didn't like to lie. He'd never liked to lie. But the time he was spending with Brie was private—it was purely their own—and he didn't have to justify his actions to his nephew, no matter how much he loved him.

Gordon returned just then with a new cup of coffee for Cyrus and a small bouquet of sweet peas, tied in pretty simplicity with a pink ribbon.

"In case you would like to give them to the young lady today," Gordon murmured.

Cyrus stiffened his shoulders and gave the other man a cool glare. Gordon had done that on purpose. Mentioned "the young lady" in front of Harrison to clue him in on the situation.

Gordon gave Cyrus a bland shrug, completely unaffected by the disapproval. "I'm sorry, sir. Shouldn't I have mentioned it?"

Harrison sat up straighter, his eyes widening in obvious surprise. "What? There's a young lady?"

"This is not a topic for public conversation," Cyrus said, his voice clipped in the way it always was when he was uncomfortable and trying to regain control of a situation.

"I'm not going to tell anyone if you don't want me to," Harrison replied, his face changing slightly. "But there's seriously a young lady? Who is she?"

"I would rather not say. It is not a... long-term situation." Cyrus chose his words very carefully. "I was told to relax and enjoy myself this month, so that's what I'm doing."

It took a minute for Harrison to process everything, but when he did, he gave a little nod. He'd always been thoughtful and discreet, and he obviously wasn't going to push the topic at the moment. He finally asked softly, "So everything is all right?"

"Yes. It is."

Harrison glanced up at Gordon, who was lingering.

Gordon gave a brief nod. "It is, sir."

Gordon's answer obviously was the one that convinced and relieved Harrison. He leaned back in his chair, sipping his coffee. Then he finally gave a little smile. "You should definitely give her the sweet peas."

~

By lunch time, Brie was on a rather foolish, romantic high.

She'd met up with Cyrus midmorning, and since it was her turn to plan the day's excursions, they'd strolled through a number of little craft shops and a huge flea market. They'd had a great time, discussing the merchandise and laughing about the tackier items. Cyrus kept buying her pretty things. Since they were all inexpensive and since he was so discreet and unassuming about it, she hadn't had the heart to object.

So she had a bag full of lovely little trinkets, a pretty bouquet of flowers he'd given her, and an excellent lunch of chicken salad in the most delicious puff pastry she'd ever eaten.

With the addition of an excellent white wine and the admiring look in Cyrus's eyes, she was well on her way to pure giddiness.

She couldn't help but notice that something had been distracting Cyrus during lunch though.

"Is something wrong?" she finally asked out of the blue.

"Of course not."

"Then why do you keep glaring at the table?"

Cyrus gave a soft chuckle, his expression softening. "I hadn't realized I was glaring."

"Well, you were."

He cleared his throat and hesitated for a moment. Then he reached over to the vase on the table—in which were stuffed an ungainly arrangement of carnations and baby's breath. He pulled out all but one sprig of the baby's breath and all the red carnations, leaving only two smaller pink-orange ones.

She stared in surprise as he calmly dropped the flowers he'd removed on an adjacent table. "That hideous arrangement was annoying me," he murmured, amused irony clear in his voice.

She burst into laughter at his actions and his expression.

His eyes narrowed as in mock reproach. "Laugh if you must, but isn't that so much better?"

"Yes," she admitted, vaguely amazed at how much lovelier the whole table looked with the few simple flowers left in the vase. "It's much better. You're kind of a perfectionist, aren't you?"

He arched his eyebrows as he took a sip of wine. "I believe those who know me would say that the word perfectionist doesn't quite do me justice."

"You're not that bad," she said, speaking honestly in response to his admission. "You haven't seemed unreasonable at all this week."

"I haven't been myself this week. Usually I hold the world to unreasonably high standards." He let out a breath, conveying an emotion she couldn't quite read. "And I hold myself to the highest standards of all."

"I don't think that's a bad thing," she said. "I think more men should hold themselves to higher standards."

His eyes returned to her face, his brief mood transforming into interest. "Are you speaking of any man in particular?"

"My ex-boyfriend. Chase."

"He didn't hold himself to high standards?"

"He didn't hold himself to any standards at all."

"How long were you with him?"

"Almost six months." She sighed, feeling bleak and stupid for a moment at the memory of that six-month error in judgment on her part.

"That's a long time to be with a man with no standards at all." Cyrus's voice was soft, cautious, as if he were being careful in how he approached the conversation.

It was clear he wanted to know about Chase though, and Brie wanted to tell him—even though it would make her look as stupid as she'd ever been.

"It was a mistake from the very beginning. He... Well, I guess he knew all the right lines. And he knew how to use his looks and attitude. I thought he was sexy and exciting, but all he was really was selfish. He took what he wanted from the

45

relationship without really offering me anything in return. And I went along with it—because anytime I tried to express my unhappiness, he would somehow charm me into forgetting it." She stared down at her nearly empty plate. "I believe in forgiveness and second chances—I really do—but he totally took advantage of that characteristic in me. I can't believe I was so stupid. I mean, I don't think I'm a stupid woman, but I sure was with him."

"So how did it end?" Cyrus asked.

"I finally just came to my senses and saw how he was treating me. He didn't cheat on me—at least as far as I know—but he did exactly what he wanted without thought to what was good for me. He lived in my apartment, letting me pay for pretty much everything. He stayed out late with his friends and never told me when he was coming home. He would... he would wake me up in the middle of the night to have sex even though he knew I had to get up in a few hours for work. He was just... selfish. And a superficial sexiness just doesn't go far enough to mask that kind of treatment for long."

"No. I would think not." Cyrus was scowling very slightly as if he were trying to rein in his negative opinion of Chase.

"So I kicked him out. It was hard. Ending a relationship that lasts so long is always hard, and he just made it worse. He wouldn't leave me alone. He kept trying to get me to take him back. My brother finally had to threaten him with a restraining order if he didn't back off. It was terrible. But I felt so much better about myself and about the world after it was over."

"It sounds like you're much better without him."

"No question about that."

They smiled at each other across the table, and Brie felt like Cyrus had heard and understood her again—which was something that had never happened with Chase.

"What about you?" she asked after a minute.

"What about me?"

"Have you had any really bad relationships?"

"Not like that. I haven't dated much at all for a long time."

"Why not?"

He was an attractive, intelligent man, and he clearly had enough money to attract a number of women even if he hadn't had other things going for him. She just couldn't understand why women weren't beating down his door.

"My life has been about working for a really long time."

This seemed to match with her impressions of him. He was obviously taking a break this week, but he seemed like the kind of man who would intently focus on his job—whatever that job happened to be. "Have you ever been married?"

"Yes. When I was very young."

She wasn't surprised. A man his age would likely to have been married before. "What happened?"

"She left me."

"Why?"

"She said it was because I was too invested in my work, and there was some truth to that. But more than that, I think she just wanted someone other than me." He glanced away as if seeing something that wasn't actually in the room. "The marriage ended when I was twenty-six, so it was a long time ago."

"And you haven't been married since?"

"No." His eyes slanted up to her face as if checking her expression. "I did date on and off through my thirties and forties. But then I had... a lot of family issues to deal with, and then my work started growing more demanding. I just didn't have time or energy... or the will to focus on another relationship. My life felt full enough without it."

"Do you still feel that way?"

"I don't know." His shoulders rose and fell in a long breath. "Honestly, I've felt at loose ends lately. My nephews have all married and are starting families of their own. My sister has a huge social circle here in Savannah. Sometimes it feels like I've been... left behind."

"Wow," she breathed, a tension aching in her chest. "I sometimes feel exactly the same way. As if everyone else has found life, and I'm just treading water, watching other people's ships go by."

He chuckled. "That's an excellent way of expressing it." He reached over and covered her hand with his. "I'm glad I'm not the only one who feels that way."

Their eyes met again but now with a deeper emotion. And Brie was starting to resent the table, which was keeping her apart from him.

She wanted to touch him, more than just their hands. She wanted to kiss him the way they'd been doing the evening before.

She wanted to do even more.

But he made no further moves, just kept his hand resting over hers. It was a strange sort of intimacy—more emotional than physical—and Brie had never really experienced it before.

It excited her. And also scared her.

She would need to keep remembering that what was happening between her and Cyrus could only last this one week.

~

A couple of hours later they were drinking coffee in an outdoor café, and Cyrus was trying to remind himself that he just had this one week with Brie.

He'd enjoyed today even more than the day before, and it was just halfway over. He wondered if each day with Brie would keep getting better.

Brie was moaning her delight over a gooey pastry he'd bought her, when a crowd started to gather across the street.

"What's that?" Brie asked, wiping her mouth with a napkin.

He shook his head. "Looks like a tour or something." He wondered what kind of delusional tourists would waste their time on a guided tour, paying good money to be herded around like sheep.

"Oh, I wonder where to." She craned her neck around to look at the tourism booth across the street.

They hadn't been having a particularly deep conversation—just occasionally making random comments— but Cyrus had been having an excellent time, watching Brie lick her lips around the pastry and seeing her brown hair and fair skin shining in the luminous sunlight.

It was a warm, sunny day. It might be December, but Savannah had never cared about the restraints of a calendar. It offered days like this all through the year.

She stood up unexpectedly. "I'm going to see what it is."

"Why?" Cyrus asked, frowning up at her.

"Just curious."

He shook his head with an amused smile as she hurried across the street. She was a rather nosy, spontaneous woman, but he liked that about her. He wondered if she had any idea how incredibly tempting her rounded, swinging hips were.

He was imagining what they might do this evening—and telling himself not to let his mind stray in dangerous directions—when Brie came back. To his surprise, she leaned over his chair with an alluring smile. "Thanks for the coffee and pastry," she said huskily. Then she captured his mouth with a soft kiss.

Cyrus responded automatically, one of his hands lifting to curve around the back of her head and his tongue sliding along her lips. He could taste the honey from the pastry. His body immediately tightened in pleasure.

She pulled back, still smiling. And while he was dazed from the kiss, she pulled him up out of his chair. "Come on."

"Where are we going?" he asked, falling in step beside her.

"The tour is visiting a nearby winery and plantation. It looks like fun, and it leaves in fifteen minutes."

"What? If you want to go see it, we can take a car."

"That's not as fun," she insisted. "The tour ends with a wine tasting."

"I can arrange a wine—"

"Cyrus, you're missing the point. I want to go on the tour."

Cyrus groaned as he looked at the gathered crowds—including elderly couples outfitted with fanny packs, sloppy children sucking on candy, college-aged kids who couldn't keep their hands off each other. "Brie," he said, trying to stage a hasty retreat. "You can't be serious."

"I am," she said cheerfully, dragging him over to buy tickets. "It's my day for choosing our activities."

With a sinking feeling that he was trapped, Cyrus gave it one more try. "Brie, it's a bus tour!"

She looked up at him with a blissful expression. "I know. Won't it be fun?"

~

The bus ride to the winery was every bit as bad as Cyrus had feared.

While the bus itself was in decent shape, it hardly compared to the comfort and luxury of his normal means of transportation. A tour guide, with an annoying penchant for making bad jokes, rambled on about the landscape and sites they happened to pass. Directly behind them sat a young couple with an infant who insisted on screaming in Cyrus's ear for most of the ride. And across the bus aisle from him was a talkative elderly woman who decided he needed to hear every agonizing detail of all her various health woes.

The only thing that saved the ride from being a complete disaster was that Brie sat beside him and became deliciously touchy. Of course, it was as he was gritting his teeth over the baby's screaming that she decided to wrap an arm around his waist and press herself up against his side. And it was in the middle of the elderly woman's dissertation on her upper GI that Brie decided to massage the back of his neck. So Cyrus didn't have focus to respond appropriately.

When the one-hour drive to the winery was finally over, they were herded off the bus and, after a brief introduction, were allowed to explore the plantation and vineyards. Cyrus immediately steered Brie away from the masses, and he actually had a decent time wandering the fields with her. While the place was overdone with less-than-historical details in order to please tourists, the day was lovely and the vineyards charming.

Brie appeared to genuinely enjoy herself, asking questions and gushing about the scenery. Cyrus knew the answers to most of her questions, and he made up answers to the ones he didn't. His cool, dry commentary made her giggle.

When she took his hand as they strolled, Cyrus felt a little odd. The gesture made him feel young and weirdly conscious of his body at the same time. He couldn't remember the last time he'd held someone's hand, except last night when it was the only safe way he'd been able to touch Brie without going too far. He never imagined such a simple, innocuous gesture would pull him so far out of his comfort zone.

More than once on the walk he began to pull his hand away. But he never quite did.

At the scheduled time, they returned to the main house for the wine tasting. Cyrus kept Brie entertained with his under-the-breath remarks on the mediocre samples they were given and the clueless, pretentious visitors who pretended to know something about wine. His particular target was an obnoxious middle-aged man who'd complained for most of the trip and who tried to lord his superiority in oenology over the rest of the group.

When the guide asked Cyrus for his opinion of one of the wine selections, Cyrus was prompted by a frivolous bit of inspiration. Keeping his expression sober, he launched into a long, imaginative description of the aroma, texture, balance and back notes, and he used every piece of wine-tasting vocabulary he had at his disposal. The result was impressive, and almost no one (including the obnoxious man) seemed to realize that it was absolute nonsense.

As he graciously acknowledged the guide's praise and the awed looks from their fellow tourists, Cyrus darted a quick look over to check Brie's expression.

Her gray eyes were huge and glowing with pure delight. And she was fighting to keep her lush lips from twitching in helpless amusement.

For a moment Cyrus felt like a teenager again—ridiculously proud of himself for earning the admiration of a pretty girl.

After the wine tasting was over, they had a half hour before the bus left to return to Savannah. Citing too much wine, Brie went to stand in line for the lady's room. Cyrus wandered over to lean on the rail of a balcony and stare out at the landscape, which was lovely even in December.

It hadn't been a bad day, really. Just a weird day. And the accumulation of unexpected moments left him feeling at loose ends, like he wasn't quite the self he'd always been comfortable with.

When he felt a hand on his lower back, he smiled and turned to greet Brie.

Except the woman touching him wasn't Brie.

Cyrus blinked, vaguely recognizing the attractive blonde as one of the members of their tour. She was tall, slim, and very tanned, and she looked to be in her midforties.

Cyrus just raised his eyebrows at her. "Did you need something?"

"You looked lonely," the woman said, standing far too close to Cyrus. "Feel like some company?"

He almost gaped, he was so surprised. She was obviously coming on to him. And while Cyrus never doubted his ability to gain the attention of a woman when he was in his element, at the moment he wasn't at his best. Someone had dribbled wine on his trousers, his shoes were dirty from the fields, and his shirt was sticking to his back from perspiration.

The woman must be insane.

Or else she knew who he was.

"I have company, thank you." He gave her a polite smile and nodded in the direction of the bathrooms.

She made a face. "The brunette? I don't see a wedding ring. And she's way too young and inexperienced for you. You can definitely do better." With a sultry look, she trailed a hand down Cyrus's back.

Cyrus was half-annoyed and half-amused, although he was convinced now that she'd recognized him as a billionaire, which was the only thing that could have prompted her ridiculously bold advance. He wasn't remotely tempted, but he was fascinated by the idea that someone would use a half-day tour as a means of finding a man. "I'm not interested," he began, starting to remove the woman's hand from where it was getting far too low on his back.

He didn't get a chance to finish his sentence or remove the woman's hand. Instead, he was grabbed and swung around so that his back was pushed against the railing.

Then a soft, lush body was pushed against his front. "Excuse me," Brie said, giving the woman a hard, narrowed-eyed glare. She then grabbed the back of Cyrus's head and pulled him down into a kiss.

Taken by surprise, Cyrus didn't respond immediately, simply let Brie tug on his lower lip and then flutter her tongue just inside his mouth. When his mind finally caught up, he wrapped his arms around her and pressed her breasts tightly against his chest before he slid one of his hands up to tangle in her long hair.

He was too distracted to pay much attention, but he was vaguely conscious of the blonde flouncing off in a snit.

When they were alone on the balcony, Brie released his head and pulled back. "The nerve of that tramp," she huffed, her cheeks rosy and eyes blazing.

Cyrus just chuckled.

Brie scowled at him. "Sure, you think it's funny. You probably liked it. And I didn't see any signs of your removing her hand from your ass."

"I was about to," he insisted, trying to subdue his amusement.

"Right. I'll have you know, Cyrus, that you're with me today. So don't be getting ideas of sneaking off behind a grapevine with a trampy, ass-grabbing blonde."

Cyrus couldn't even be offended by the implication. Her words were obviously prompted by jealousy—something that thrilled Cyrus to no end. And the hint of insecurity that Brie had revealed made his own minor uncertainties today far more palatable. Stroking his fingers through her soft hair, he murmured, "I know I'm with you. I have no desire to be with anyone else."

Brie sniffed a little. "Oh. Good."

"Brie?" Cyrus asked softly, moving a hand forward so he could rub one her cheekbones with his thumb.

"What?" She avoided his gaze although she had her hands fisted in his shirt.

"Brie, were you actually jealous?" His heart was beating with ludicrous speed as hope, excitement, and desire started to course through his body with his blood.

"Of course not. I was annoyed. She was just being rude and inappropriate."

"Not even a little jealous?"

"Well, how would you feel if some guy came along and was feeling me up when you were just in the bathroom for a few minutes."

"I would be quite angry." He knew it was the truth, and he had to acknowledge that it meant certain things about his feelings for Brie that he never would have expected.

"So we're in the same boat then." She looked up at him, partly self-conscious and partly deeply sincere. "We're with only each other this week."

"Agreed." He tried to fight against his physical response to her closeness, but he felt himself hardening just a little—which was both surprising and completely inappropriate—and he couldn't quite even out his breathing.

And he was starting to wonder if it would really be so wrong to give in to his feelings for Brie, if only for this week.

Four

The next morning, Brie checked herself out in the mirror of her room at Mitchell and Deanna's house.

She wore another long cotton skirt—this time in a lovely brown and rose floral print—and a casual top that made the most of her breasts, which she admittedly could only do so much for since they weren't her most impressive feature.

She thought she looked pretty though. As pretty as she was capable of looking.

It might not be enough to get Cyrus into bed though.

They'd eaten dinner on the way back from the vineyard, and he'd held her hand as they'd walked to her car in the dark. Then he'd kissed her—not quite so gently as he had the evening before. She'd been so completely into him that she wouldn't have hesitated at all had he invited her to his place for the night.

He hadn't though.

She knew it wasn't because he didn't want her. She'd felt very clearly in his body that he wanted her. He was a lot older than her, but he wasn't *that* old.

But something else was holding him back.

Maybe he wasn't the kind of man who would consider sex in a situation like theirs—when there wasn't any future to offer. He was rather old-fashioned about a lot of things. She certainly knew that by now. She liked it about him.

She would also like to have sex though.

But she wasn't going to try to jump him. She knew instinctively that would never work on a man like Cyrus. He came across as calm and unassuming, but he had a really strong will and an air of authority that sometimes surprised her.

She wondered what he did for work. He must have advanced to a fairly high level, whatever it was. He just had that sense about him—like he was used to always being in control of the room.

She cleared her thoughts, reminding herself that his job and the rest of his life didn't really matter. They'd met on Monday, and now it was Friday. The week was almost over.

If she was ever going to have sex with him, it would have to be soon.

It would be a deep disappointment in her life if she never got the chance.

With a sigh, she leaned over to dig her shoes out of the closet—velvet ballet slippers in the same shade of brown as her skirt. Before she could slide them on, though, there was a knock on her door.

"Brie?" Deanna's voice came through the closed door.

"Come on in."

As the door swung open, Deanna continued, "Do you want to come Christmas shopping with me and Rose tod—" She broke off her words as she saw Brie.

Deanna's sister Rose was standing beside her in the hall, pretty and curvy and smiling sweetly.

"Hi, Rose," Brie said with a smile. "Good to see you. I'm sorry I can't go shopping with you today. I already have plans."

"With your mystery man?" Deanna's grin was mischievous now.

"Ooh, there's a mystery man?" Rose looked from her sister to Brie.

"There's no mystery man! I mean, it's nothing serious."

"You look awfully pretty today for it to be nothing serious," Deanna said, eyeing Brie from head to toe.

"And you painted your toenails," Rose chimed in.

Brie sighed as she looked down at her bare feet and pretty pink toenails. She'd done a lot more than that this morning as she got ready.

If Cyrus was going to see her naked today—which might be a long shot but was still a possibility—she wanted to look as perfect as possible.

"I'm trying to keep it in perspective," Brie explained. "We're just hanging out for the week. It's not ever going to go anywhere."

Deanna and Rose looked at each other. "It doesn't really work very well," Deanna said slowly. "Trying to keep things with a guy in perspective, even when you know better. At least in my experience."

"My experience too," Rose agreed. "That's the thing about the heart. It doesn't understand perspective."

"Well, mine's going to have to." Brie put on her shoes and then squared her shoulders. "I'm not letting myself hope or dream of anything else beyond this week."

"Okay. I hope that works out for you then." Deanna didn't sound convinced, but her smile was supportive and Brie figured that was the best she could expect.

It didn't matter if no one else understood. She and Cyrus understood.

She was doing what she wanted this month. And she wanted to spend as much time as possible with him—even if it never went anywhere.

~

They went out for brunch, but neither one was in a very energetic mood, so they agreed to go back to Cyrus's house and just hang out for the afternoon.

If Brie was hoping that "hanging out" would mean sex, she was disappointed however. They lounged together on the big chaise in the garden, talking about books. Then they went inside to watch an old British film that both of them enjoyed. Cyrus wrapped his arm around her shoulders, and she leaned against him, but he didn't deepen the embrace beyond a few kisses brushed into her hair.

And she loved it. All of it. But she was starting to wonder if Cyrus just wasn't interested in sex with her. His body might want it, but obviously none of the rest of him did.

At least not enough.

It was okay. It wasn't the end of the world. She loved being with him even if it didn't involve sex.

But she also wanted to have sex with him.

More every hour she spent with him.

The movie ended at about four thirty, and they stayed together on the sofa, sitting in companionable silence. Cyrus would occasionally run a hand down her hair, and she really liked the feeling.

She liked the feel of his body beside her too. He was in good shape for a man his age, but he wasn't particularly big or athletic. But she liked the lean hardness of him, the way every part of his body seemed to be warm. She liked the gentleness of his hands. He never touched her without making her feel very special.

She wondered what it would feel like if he touched her intimately, then decided it was probably better not to think of that at the moment.

"Is there anything you'd like to do now?" Cyrus asked after a few minutes.

She didn't lift her head from where it was pressing against his chest. "I don't know. I don't really feel like going out."

"Me either. Gordon can make us dinner later if you'd like."

"That sounds good."

For a moment she felt his lips against her hair again, but they were gone before she could turn her head to check. She told herself not to push it, that he wasn't the kind of man who would like to feel pressured. But she heard herself saying anyway, "Cyrus?"

"Yes, dear heart?"

She adjusted enough so she could look him in the face, her heart leaping excitedly at the old-fashioned endearment. "I..." She trailed off, unsure of how to say what she evidently was going to say.

"What is it, Brie?" He gently caressed her cheek with his knuckles, his lovely brown eyes very soft.

She swallowed hard. "I wouldn't mind... I mean, I would like to be... even closer to you if that's something you want."

For just a moment he grew very still.

"I'd understand if you're not interested," she said hurriedly, feeling her cheeks start to burn. "If I'm not really your type, or if that's not what you were thinking about us. I just..." She ended with a ragged little breath.

"Brie," he said, straightening up and then cupping her face in both his hands. "Of course I want to. Surely you can see that I do. But you have to understand, this isn't something I usually do. Outside of relationships, I've never.... done anything. I suppose that strikes you as obscenely old-fashioned."

"No, not at all!" Of course he wasn't the kind of man who had casual sex. She never would have believed he was. "I understand. It's fine if it's too soon or if you'd rather not—I mean, with someone you're just spending time with for the week. I like just being with you. I just wanted to let you know... let you know... I'm willing."

She gulped at how stupid she must have sounded.

Something had come alive in his eyes, though, in the middle of her rambles. Something that made her realize he hadn't thought she'd sounded stupid at all.

"You really want to?" he murmured.

"Well, yeah." She blinked in surprise. Because she was surprised, the truth came tumbling out. "I've never wanted to have sex with any other man as much as I want to have sex with you."

She heard his breath hitch very slightly. A look that was almost awed had arisen in his eyes. It completely took her breath away. "And I've never wanted anyone the way I want you, Brie."

Her eyes glazed over with a rush of feeling, and she knew he was going to kiss her. She was leaning into it, wanting it desperately, when there was a tap from the doorway.

Both of them jerked and turned to see Gordon.

"I'm very sorry, sir," Gordon said, his eyes focused downward. "But you have a call from your nephew. The eldest. It sounds important, or I never would have interrupted you."

It took a moment for Cyrus to shift gears. Brie could see the transformation on his face—from the hot softness in his gaze to something concerned and professional. "I'm so sorry, dear heart," he murmured, leaning forward to give her quick kiss. "My nephew works with me. It must be important."

"Of course. Go take it."

She was disappointed—deeply—at the interruption of the intensity of the moment before, but she wasn't annoyed. He couldn't help it if something important had come up.

She watched as Cyrus left the room, and then she leaned back against the couch.

When Cyrus returned, they were going to have sex. She was almost sure they would. Her heart raced with excitement, and her belly twisted at the same time.

She wanted it. So much.

She just hoped it wouldn't make things so much harder next week when all this was over.

She waited for twenty minutes, growing more worried by whatever had prompted the phone call, when her eyes slanted over to the doorway and saw Gordon, who was waiting quietly for her to notice him.

"Can I get you anything, miss?" he asked.

"No. I don't think so. Is everything all right with Cyrus? I mean, with the call."

"It was an emergency," he explained. "Work related but serious. I'm afraid he might be a while longer."

Her brows drew together. "Is it really serious?"

"I'm sure he can take care of it. Perhaps you'd like to do something else while you wait."

Brie looked around aimlessly. She had no idea what she wanted to do.

"You mentioned the hot tub yesterday," Gordon suggested. "You would be welcome to make use of it if you'd like."

"Oh, I'd love to, but I didn't bring a suit." She wished she had. The hot tub sounded wonderful right about now.

"You could have as much privacy as you'd like."

Brie hesitated just briefly. Then she nodded. "Okay. Thank you."

She'd brought a change of underwear with her—just in case she spent the night with Cyrus. She would feel too exposed wearing nothing in the hot tub, but there was no reason not to wear her bra and panties. It wouldn't be that much different from a bikini.

And if Cyrus would happen to come to join her, then all the better.

~

There had been an accident during the preparations for the launch of the tearoom, and someone had gotten hurt.

It wasn't something that normally happened in Cyrus's line of work, so he and Harrison were both disturbed and rattled by the event. When he'd gotten the details from Harrison, he made several calls and then called Harrison back to talk through what should happen next.

Eventually the aftermath of the accident was taken care of and the news from the hospital was good. He blinked absently when Gordon tapped on the office door.

"Everything all right?" Cyrus asked, rubbing his eyes and starting to wonder about Brie. He'd left her at the worst possible time.

"Yes, sir. Are you aware that it's after seven?"

Cyrus blinked again. "What? It can't be. Wasn't it just before five when I came in here?"

"Yes, sir."

"What about Brie?"

"She is making do."

Cyrus groaned as he realized what happened. He'd lived on his own for so long that he had a bad habit of losing track of time and focusing completely on work to the detriment of everything else. "Was she upset?"

Gordon dropped his eyes. "She wasn't expecting for you to be busy for so long."

"Damn." He rarely swore, but it was the only word that suited his feelings at the moment.

"I've prepared a dinner that can be served at room temperature, so you can eat it whenever you'd like. I also put some red wine out," Gordon said, falling in step beside Cyrus as he headed out of the office. "But if you would prefer champagne—"

"Wine is good, thanks." Cyrus looked into the lounge, where he'd last seen Brie, but the room was empty. He could see outside that the sun had set.

He'd lost far too much time when he only had a limited amount of time to spend with her at all.

"Where is she?" Cyrus asked.

"I believe she might have stepped outside."

"All right. Thank you." He reached for one of the French doors that led to the patio, not wanting to waste any time in finding her.

"If I might be so bold, sir," Gordon began.

Cyrus's lip twitched, despite his concern for Brie. "Did you pick that line up from an old British mystery?"

Amusement flashed briefly in Gordon's eyes. "Of course, sir."

"What was it you were going to say?" Cyrus was getting impatient to go out to Brie, his body already tensing with anticipation. But he would never be rude to someone as invaluable and faithful as Gordon.

"It wouldn't be a bad idea for you to shower first."

Cyrus's lips parted slightly as he processed Gordon's words. Glancing down at himself, he realized he'd sweated some in his urgency before, and he looked hot and wrinkled. Not exactly the condition he'd prefer for his first night with Brie. "Oh. Right."

"And I have other provisions, should you need them."

Cyrus had no idea what provisions Gordon was talking about. His world had boiled down to two things.

Shower first. Then Brie.

~

Had he been thinking more clearly, Cyrus would have noticed that there were clothes that weren't his draped over one of the chairs in the master bedroom.

That fact hardly registered in his mind though. He was thinking about Brie, by herself outside. Waiting for him.

Probably wondering if he wanted her at all.

He would have to show her how much he did want her.

He opened the bathroom door and stepped inside, jerking to a stop when he realized there was someone in the shower.

Brie was in the shower.

The shower was large, beautifully tiled, and made so it didn't need a shower curtain or door, so he could see her very clearly as the water poured down over her from the rainfall showerhead.

Water streamed over her bare flesh. Her arms were lifted to wring water out of her long hair, a position that lifted her firm breasts in a tantalizing way. Her fair skin looked luminous in the artificial light, broken only by the darkened tips of her nipples. Her eyes were closed, and she hadn't yet seen him.

The fact that she was unaware of his presence made the sight even more alluring. She was completely unselfconscious, her motion not intended to be seductive as she pulled the water out of her hair, causing her breasts to bounce a little.

Cyrus grew hard as he stood watching, so quickly it actually hurt. He'd never seen anyone—anything—that he wanted with such an intense, visceral hunger.

His eyes raked over her dripping, naked flesh, devouring the sight of her lush breasts, smooth belly, and rosy, erect nipples. His eyes returned to her face and saw the moment she recognized his presence.

"God!" she gasped, covering herself with one arm in an automatic gesture of defense.

His mind finally caught up, and he turned on his heel quickly, showing her his back. "I'm sorry. I'm sorry. Gordon said you were outside."

"I was. It's fine," Brie said, her voice strangely hoarse. "You just startled me. I was outside—Gordon said I could use the hot tub. But then I wanted to take a shower, and I thought it would be okay since you were still working. I'm sorry—"

"Don't be sorry. It's not your fault. I'm sorry to just walk in like that." He wasn't really sorry. He couldn't stop visualizing Brie's gorgeous dripping body behind him, and his body was responding to that luscious vision.

Responding quite dramatically.

"Is everything all right with work?" she asked. He heard the shower water turn off.

"Yes. It is now. It was an emergency. I apologize for leaving you alone so long."

"You don't have to apologize. But you took care of everything?"

"Yes."

"And there's nothing to worry about now?"

"No. Nothing."

"Good. So you can turn around, Cyrus," Brie said in a different tone.

"It's probably not a good idea."

"I think it would be a good idea. I think it would be a *very* good idea."

"Brie."

"You know what I want. And I think you want it too. And honestly, Cyrus, I'm starting to get a little impatient." She paused for a moment. "I would completely understand if you're not comfortable with this, given that we're not in a relationship. But it sounded earlier like you might be okay with it. So what are you waiting for?"

He wasn't sure what he was waiting for. Maybe for the heavens to open and pour out a sign that this was really all right, that he was allowed something so incredibly good, something he wanted so much.

Brie's voice behind him was as close to a sign as he was ever going to get. With a groan of relief, Cyrus turned around and took a few steps toward the shower, reaching out to draw her into a deep kiss. She was immediately urgent, opening to the advance of his tongue and eagerly rubbing herself against him.

For a moment, Cyrus thought he might drown in her passion, her sweetness, the lush life she embodied. He made a guttural sound against her mouth and felt the awakening needs of the past three days coalesce in the throbbing of his groin.

She rocked against him, her hands clutching at his shoulders, his back, his head. "Cyrus."

He grunted in response, his hands now busy sliding down her back so he could feel her bare bottom, soft and curved and lush and perfect.

"Cyrus," she rasped again.

This time, he realized she was trying to get his attention. His heart lurched as he desperately hoped she wasn't about to change her mind.

"Sex in the shower isn't exactly good for me," she said, almost sheepish.

His laugh was half amusement, half relief. "The bedroom is just a few steps away."

He reached for a towel and wrapped it around her shoulders, and they walked together into the bedroom.

The bed was large, a four-poster antique with a crisp white duvet. Moonlight streamed in through the wide windows that looked out on the garden. The bouquet of lavender and roses on the dresser filled the room with their presence. And Gordon had lit candles on the table, next to a bottle of wine and crystal glasses. While he would have been happy to have sex with Brie in any place, at any time, there was a deeply romantic aura to the setting, and he thought she would probably appreciate it.

She was gazing around with wonder in her eyes. "It's beautiful."

Cyrus pulled her into his arms.

Half in their embrace, they made their way over to tumble into the bed. Brie rolled onto her back, arching her spine as Cyrus moved over her and took one of her breasts in his mouth.

"Oh God," she groaned, her cheeks flushed and her eyes wide open as she stared up at the small crystal chandelier.

Cyrus suckled and twirled his tongue on her tight nipple, turned on even more by her responsiveness. His hands stroked over her firm, damp skin, following every delicious curve and dip he could find.

"Oh God," Brie gasped again, her arms moving above her head and clutching at the thick pillows. "So good. So... perfect." Her head tossed restlessly, and her eyes moved from Cyrus at her breast, to the big windows where a nearly full moon was visible in the dark sky.

Cyrus hummed against her breast, loving the way he felt her shudder. He released her nipple and nuzzled his way down her belly, which rose and fell quickly with her urgent breathing.

Brie alternated between stroking and clutching his head, and her pelvis was already rocking rhythmically. When he moved up to her other breast, she started to whimper, the helpless, little sound going straight to his arousal.

"Oh, Cyrus," she said hoarsely, "I want you so much."

Cyrus pulled his head up to gaze down on her. He knew she was speaking the truth. Her body writhed and rocked beneath him with her wet hair spread out under her head like a sopping halo. She was delectably flushed all the way down to her belly. And she kept trying to wrap one of her legs around his hips.

His chest throbbed nearly as deeply as his erection as he processed the reality. "Brie," he murmured, "I want you too."

He lowered his head again, determined to please her and not let his own urgency take over. It had been too long since he had done this, but it wasn't like he'd forgotten how. He mouthed a line between her breasts and back down her belly. Then he went further to nuzzle at her warm, intimate flesh.

He breathed deeply, taking in the natural scent of her arousal, which triggered a primitive impulse that made him want to howl. She started whimpering again as he nudged her open and fluttered his tongue inside her. Then she arched up dramatically with a cry of pleasure when he closed his lips around her clit.

It took almost no time at all for her body to shudder through an intense climax, a delicious moan slipping out of her lips as she let herself go.

And he couldn't believe it. Couldn't believe that he'd made her feel that way, that she wanted him to.

Brie opened her eyes and smiled up at him. "Thank you," she gasped. "Thank you. That was really generous."

He shook his head, wondering what kind of bastards she'd been with before, who wouldn't consider doing that for her as a special privilege.

"Can you reach my bag?" she asked, her expression changing.

He wasn't sure what she wanted, but he leaned down to snag the strap from the floor and handed the bag to her.

She reached into an inner pocket and pulled out a condom packet.

Of course. It had never even occurred to him.

He was woefully out of practice.

Then he realized something else. "Provisions," he muttered wryly. That was what Gordon had been talking about.

Brie couldn't possibly know what he was referring to, but her eyes sparkled anyway. "Exactly. Now tell me why you're wearing so many clothes."

He didn't have an answer for her, and she started to take care of the situation anyway. Pretty soon he was as naked as she was, and he couldn't help but see the excited admiration in her eyes.

She obviously wasn't disappointed in him. At all. In fact, her eyes were almost possessive as she rolled the condom on for him and then reached her arms out for him. "Get up here."

He moved into her embrace, positioning himself between her legs. Then he was adjusting her thigh to pull her farther open for him. And then he was lining himself up at her entrance.

And then—the world a pulsing, glowing blur around him—he was finally sinking inside her.

She released a pretty moan as the substance of him pushed inside her. She was tight. Deliciously tight. And so hot he could feel it through the condom.

"Oh God," he gasped, jerking his head to the side and holding himself perfectly still. He couldn't remember anything ever feeling so good.

"Cyrus!" Brie's arms tightened around him. And she was so eager she had already started to pump her hips, trying to get him to move inside her.

"Just a minute." He bit his lip as he tried to get his wayward body to obey the demands of his mind. He was not—not—going to spoil this by coming too soon like a teenaged boy getting lucky for the first time.

Brie mewed out her impatience but managed to hold herself still. Then, irrepressible, she quipped, only a little breathless, "I thought men your age had the opposite problem."

He choked on a burst of laughter. Finding his voice, he said, "I've always been remarkable." He even managed a suggestive twitch of his eyebrows.

She giggled and pulled him down into a soft hug. "Definitely remarkable."

A swell of tenderness and something else—something he couldn't quite identify—broke in his chest to flood his belly. He panted against her wet hair and dazedly wondered how she was doing this to him.

After a minute, he pulled himself together. Straightened his arms and pulled his chest up from hers so he'd have better leverage to thrust. Then he pulled his hips back and pitched them forward.

She gasped loudly, reaching up to dig her fingers into the back of his shoulders.

He thrust again, and this time she lifted her hips to meet his. After just a minute, they'd synchronized their motion into an urgent, carnal rhythm that seemed to mirror his deepest need. Brie knew what she was doing—her intimate muscles clenched around him deliciously, and her little hands explored his body with shameless entitlement. But all her responses, all her soft whimpers and moans, all her squirming and shaking and the growing tension of her muscles, were natural, genuine, infinitely real.

Cyrus could hear music coming from somewhere in the house, beyond the rhythmic slapping of their flesh and the mingled texture of their breathing. He could see the glow of moonlight through the window, illuminating Brie's gorgeous, wanton body rocking eagerly beneath him.

And he wondered how he had lived—lived for far too long—without experiencing this before.

"Oh God," Brie choked, her body tightening palpably, shaking in tense little shudders.

Cyrus could feel her inner muscles start to tighten around him, and his steady rhythm accelerated to urgent, hungry jerks of his hips. "Yes, dear heart. Can you come?"

"Yeah. Oh, yeah." She was shaking wildly now, had fallen out of rhythm completely. Her face twisted in pleasure, and she bit her lip hard.

Then her whole body arched up from the bed, and her mouth fell open in a silent scream. She clamped down around him so brutally Cyrus let out a muffled exclamation.

As Brie convulsed beneath him with the spasms of her climax, Cyrus lost control completely. With a series of primitive grunts, he pushed hard against her clenching muscles and felt a blinding wave of pleasure swell up and then release as he came too.

His climax was powerful, and it left him limp and speechless. He slumped down on top of Brie, oddly soothed by the way she held him in a tight embrace. She panted just as desperately as him, and her clinging body felt just as urgently hot.

Cyrus didn't want to move—never wanted to move— but he knew he had to when he felt his erection start to soften. With an agonized groan, he managed to heave himself off her and carefully pull himself out of her while holding the condom in place.

"Oh God, that was good," Brie groaned as she stretched out like a cat on the bed.

His chest swelling at this affirmation, he quickly took care of the condom and then returned to join her on the duvet.

She snuggled up against him but darted him a questioning look. "Didn't you think it was good too?"

Cyrus had to laugh at that ludicrous piece of understatement. "Of course it was good."

Stroking his bare chest, she smiled at him. "Then we'll have to do it again." When he didn't answer immediately, she prompted, "Right?"

Cyrus blinked. He was so overcome by the power of his climax that he had trouble thinking clearly. But it seemed to him that Brie was actually uncertain about whether he'd want to have sex with her again.

Could she possibly think that, now that he'd had a taste of her, he was anywhere close to satisfied?

"Right," he agreed thickly. "Again. And again. And again."

She snickered again, obviously pleased by his reply. "Well, we only have a couple more days. And you're not as young as you used to be."

Cyrus made a growling noise that surprised him. "Did you have any particular complaints?"

Brie lifted herself up, naked and luminous in the low light, and leaned down to press a sweet kiss on his mouth. "I have no complaints in the world."

He saw something in her eyes then as she gazed down on him. The expression was gone in an instant. Nothing more than a flicker that was quickly covered by ironic amusement. But Cyrus was sure he had seen it, and it took his breath away.

He didn't understand it. Didn't know what to call it. Didn't know how it was possible that Brie had looked at him with that expression. It went far deeper than lust. But wasn't simple affection as he'd always understood it.

Cyrus was who he was. And after all these years, nothing significant could really change in his soul. And there were certain things, certain experiences, that would never be a part of his life.

He knew—he had always known—the price of his wealth, the price of his scars, the price of his ambition, the price of his blood. And only a fool would believe the price could be paid.

But still he had seen something in Brie's eyes. He didn't know what to call it, but he wasn't likely to ever forget it.

She'd seen something in him he hadn't known even existed, but he was starting to wish really did.

Five

Brie woke up the following morning groggy and disoriented.

She blinked several times in the bright room and wondered where the hell she was. The sheets and duvet were all wrong, and above her, instead of the ceiling fan in her room in Mitchell's house, was decorative plaster molding and a crystal chandelier.

As her mind started to process, she remembered she'd spent yesterday at Cyrus's lovely borrowed house. There were huge windows all around her and French doors that led onto a balcony. Sun came pouring in from every angle. The sleek clock on the bedside table read 9:37.

Brie sat up abruptly, the covers falling down to her waist. She stared around her as she finally oriented herself. She was in Cyrus's bedroom. In Cyrus's bed.

And they'd had sex last night.

They'd stayed up late, even after having sex. They'd drunk wine and ate a light dinner as they lounged around and talked on the balcony. Finally, after two in the morning, Brie had been so tired she'd been about to drop. She'd fully expected to drive home, but Cyrus had silently pulled her back into bed with him to sleep.

He wasn't around now. It was fairly late in the morning, and he'd probably woken up early. Brie felt kind of silly and lonely by herself in this huge, luxurious bed. All she was wearing was the little cotton gown with lace straps she'd stuck in her bag the morning before. Sex or not, she wasn't too keen on going around completely naked. She slumped back in bed and pulled the covers back up to her shoulders.

She wondered what Cyrus was doing.

Brie felt a little twinge of soreness between her legs and felt her cheeks flush as she remembered her passion and her enthusiastic performance the night before. There was no doubt—it was the best sex she'd ever had in her life. She got a bit tingly just thinking about it.

Chase had always been like a wave of hot passion that slammed into her and then was over. With Cyrus, it was slower, deeper, longer, and just better in every way.

She gasped and sat up again in the bed as the bedroom door opened without warning. Despite the fact that she had every reason to be where she was, she still felt like an interloper, like she didn't quite belong here.

And she was embarrassed for Gordon to see her like this.

To her relief, Cyrus himself entered the room. He was dressed in a pair of soft, light-colored pajama pants, with bare chest and bare feet. The intimacy of his appearance and the way the pants rode low on his hips gave her the most unexpected feeling of ownership.

She was the only woman who got to see him like this, and she wanted it to stay that way.

He carried a tray with coffee, fruit and pastries, and he smiled when he found her awake.

"Hi," she said stupidly. "I woke up."

He chuckled and put the tray down on the bedside table. "I can see that."

"I thought you'd be busy or something."

"Busy with what? I'm on an enforced vacation, remember?" He poured her a cup of coffee, which she accepted gratefully. Then he stood by the bed with his own coffee and gazed down at her with the oddest expression. It

78

was partly fond, partly ironic, and partly amused. His lips twitched visibly as his eyes scanned over her face and body.

She frowned. "Is something wrong?"

"Of course not." He got into bed beside her and propped himself up on the pillows.

Reclining beside him, she peered at his expression. "You were laughing at me."

"I was doing nothing of the kind."

"You were too! You still are." Her mind raced over various possibilities, but she could think of nothing she'd done to prompt the teasing amusement she'd seen. "Did I snore or something?"

Laughing, he draped an arm around her and pulled her against his side. "Not that I heard."

She snuggled up against him and sipped her coffee, pleasantly surprised by his easy mood this morning. She'd wondered if he might withdraw a bit after the intensity of their lovemaking last night. "I didn't sleep in *that* late. When did you wake up?"

"Hours ago," he admitted.

"What have you been doing all this time?"

"I took a walk. Made a few calls about the issue yesterday." He handed her the basket of pastries, and she picked out a particularly decadent one.

"So everything is all right with that? No... lasting damage?" she asked after she'd swallowed her first bite.

"No lasting damage."

As much as she'd tried to be reasonable, given the fact that he'd obviously had a real work emergency, she'd been very disappointed that he'd left her alone for so long yesterday. She'd soaked in the hot tub for as long as she could handle, but then she'd finally given up on Cyrus returning to her with his mind full of sex, so she'd gotten out and gone to take a shower.

She certainly hadn't expected for him to walk in on her the way he had.

The sex had been amazing, but the delay had actually helped. The recognition that she wasn't Cyrus's priority—not even for a single day. He had a full life that had nothing to do with her. And although she knew he was seeking in her a pleasurable interlude from his real life, she needed to keep the whole thing in perspective. It was only one week. One wonderful week with Cyrus. And his forgetting about her briefly the day before as he took care of work actually helped to remind her.

Oh, he liked her. She knew that. And he was deeply attracted to her. And she'd helped to brighten this week for him—given him something new to do, to think about, to experience. But there was no chance of anything more. So she'd been able to go into their lovemaking the night before with the right attitude. And she'd made sure she enjoyed it as much as she could, knowing it would only be temporary.

In two more days, he would leave. And this time with Cyrus would be no more than the most indulgent, pleasurable holiday she'd ever had.

Cyrus had probably been able to let himself go as much as he had because he knew he would return to his old self at the end of it.

Brie wasn't a fool. There was no fairy-tale end to this unexpected encounter. She'd grown up too much to delude herself into believing there could be. She was almost thirty. She wasn't a child anymore.

She wasn't about to say no to what she was offered though. A week with Cyrus was better than nothing at all.

Realizing Cyrus was looking at her strangely, Brie blinked. "What were we saying?"

With a dry chuckle, he replied, "You were asking about my work problem, and I'd told you there was no lasting damage."

"Oh. I am glad about that."

"Me too."

They lay around and ate breakfast in companionable silence until Brie asked, "Why did you bring up the tray yourself? Shouldn't Gordon do it?"

Cyrus's eyes had slipped down from her face to her bare arms and shoulders, then lingered on the outline of her breasts and tight nipples through the thin cotton. "I think it's better that no one but me gets to see you like this."

Brie's whole body clenched at the implications of his words, but she managed to say lightly, "That was an excellent answer, but I don't believe you. Gordon would never leer at me. Why did you really bring it up?"

"I was down there and coming up anyway." Cyrus gave a matter-of-fact shrug. "Why ask Gordon to make an extra trip?"

For some reason, the slight discomfort in his eyes—as if he was actually a bit embarrassed about looking out for the well-being of his staff, even in such a minor way—made Brie feel absurdly tender. To cover it, she asked, "Tell me about Gordon. Where did you find him?"

"I found him through a referral," he said, thoughtfully chewing on a grape. "I've never been more grateful."

"What's his background?" Brie had grown to like and respect the quiet man, and she was genuinely curious.

"I don't know the whole story. He's intensely private. He's British, and his father was in charge of the domestic staff at a huge estate in the Cotswolds. Gordon's wife had died the year before I hired him, and I think he was looking for something new."

"Oh." Brie frowned, saddened by this unexpected detail about Gordon's life.

"His role here is more than a servant," Cyrus added.

"I know that." Studying Cyrus's face, she realized something she hadn't known before. He didn't just like and respect Gordon as an employee. Cyrus considered him part of the family.

It was just a random detail. But for some reason, the knowledge touched Brie deeply.

She'd assumed that was all he was willing to share with her for the moment, but then he went on. "I had two older brothers, and both of them and their wives died suddenly when their sons were children."

"Oh my God!" she breathed, horrified by the thought, by how quickly his family had broken apart like that. "What happened?"

"It was an... accident. But because of it two of my nephews came to stay with me."

"Really? Was that after your wife left?"

"Yes. I was single then. I wasn't remotely prepared to raise children, and I never would have made it without Gordon."

"That must have been so hard for you—to take care of little boys."

"It wasn't easy. But it was more difficult for the boys." He sighed and slumped back slightly against the pillows. "I didn't do a good job with the role. I was more like a... dictator than an uncle. I should have done a lot better by them."

"I'm sure they don't think so. You seem close to them now."

He slanted her a curious look. "You think so?"

Suddenly embarrassed for no good reason, she ducked her head briefly. "I don't know. Just from the few things I've heard you mention about them, it seems like you're close to them. If I can pick up that you love them after just a few days. I'm sure they know it too."

"I hope so," he murmured. "We've gotten closer in the past few years. I've... done better, I think. I hope they know it now. They mean the world to me."

The words caused Brie's heart to ache in her chest with a feeling she couldn't possibly process. Having no choice but to act on the depth of her tenderness, she reached over to take Cyrus's coffee mug out of his hand and put both his and hers on the nightstand.

Then Brie moved over him, straddling his lap as he lounged against the thick pillows.

Cyrus's eyes widened in pleasure and surprise. "I guess that means you've had enough breakfast."

She smiled at him with her best seductive look. "More than enough. How are you feeling?"

"I feel fine. What do you mean?"

"I mean, is it too soon for you? Are you up to... enjoying the morning this way?" She really had no idea how he would respond. Obviously she knew men his age slowed down when it came to sex, but she had no idea what that would look like or how it would work itself out in any individual man. She didn't want to be insensitive and push.

He chuckled. "I believe I can summon the fortitude, given the temptation and reward."

Giggling at his choice of words, she kissed him, tasting coffee on his lips and the slight tang of grapes.

His arms moved around her immediately, pulling her tightly against his chest. They kissed for a long time, slowly, deeply, moving their mouths against each other and sliding their tongues together. His body was warm and hard under hers, and she loved the feel of his firm flesh against her skin. Irresistibly drawn, she moved her hands to his hair so she could tangle her fingers into it.

After a few minutes, his body began to tense beneath her more palpably, and she felt his erection growing against her, matching her own deepening arousal. He tore his mouth away and grabbed the fabric of her gown so he could pull it over her head. She was wearing nothing underneath.

She was both thrilled and self-conscious at the heat and possessiveness in his eyes as he stared at her naked body. Before she could think of anything witty or ironic to say to break the tension, he lifted her up by the waist until he could take one of her breasts in his mouth.

She moaned as he teased her into hotter, wetter arousal. His mouth and tongue were skillful, and Brie already felt overly sensitized to every one of his touches. When his fondling became delicious torture, she pulled away and yanked down his pajama pants.

His erection freed, she took him in both hands, loving the feel of him, this evidence of his wanting her so much. She stroked him with her thumbs—then rubbed her palm in small circles over the head of his shaft. He jerked at her first touch and then made the sexiest, guttural sound she'd ever heard.

After a minute, he pulled her hands away by the wrist and reached over to the nightstand to grab a condom, where she'd put the extras from her bag last night. When he'd rolled it on, he silently positioned her above him, and she exhaled with pleasure as she sank down to sheathe him with her body.

He reached out to gather her into another deep kiss as she began to rock slowly. The rhythm of their kiss soon matched the rhythm of their bodies, and Brie was shocked that something so simple, a motion so gentle, could bring her to orgasm so quickly.

But after only a few minutes, her muscles started to tense, and she grew very tight around his penetration. She dropped her head back, breaking off the kiss at last. She panted out with silly huffs of effort and pleasure as she rode Cyrus more urgently.

She felt his eyes on her—still hot and possessive—as she bounced on his lap until the tension at her center finally unleashed. She bit off her cry of release as the spasms of sensation pulsed through her, and then she slumped forward toward his chest.

His hands slid up from her bare hips to wrap around her back. He kissed her again, hungry and almost clumsy as his steady rocking beneath her shifted to faster, harder bucks of his hips. Her intimate muscles were exquisitely tight, exquisitely sensitive after her climax. And she could feel him moving inside her, could hear the shameless, wet sounds from the connection of their flesh.

Panting against his mouth, Brie squeezed a hand down between their bodies until she could rub her clit. She whimpered at the resulting sensations, and Cyrus groaned into the kiss as her muscles contracted even more around him.

She rubbed herself hard and followed Cyrus's rhythm as he bucked up into her from below. He soon fell out of rhythm, and his body clenched like a fist. Then he came in a series of jerks and long, thick grunts. Brie massaged her clit as frantically as she could, pushing herself into climax again at the very last moment.

They'd lost the kiss when they came, although their mouths were still so close they bumped against each other as their bodies convulsed. Brie bit her lower lip to stifle the scream her body demanded, so the sound of her release came out as a childish mew.

She collapsed on Cyrus, who was still propped up on the pillows. Sated and exhausted, she panted against his neck and tried not to think about the fact that she'd never see him again after tomorrow.

Cyrus held her for a few moments, but then he nudged at her gently so he could pull out and take care of the condom.

She stifled her groan of reluctance as she rolled off him. They hadn't spoken since their first kiss.

He disposed of the condom and then came back to bed, giving her a pleased, warm look. "I wasn't expecting that this morning."

A burst of laughter broke out of her. "Honestly, I wasn't either."

He took her into his arms so she was leaning against him. "What do you want to do today?"

She smiled against his chest. "I don't know."

"I need to have tea with my sister this afternoon. She'll be expecting me."

"That's fine. I'm sure I can amuse myself for a couple of hours."

"I don't actually like spending those hours away from you. We have so little time as it is." He pressed a light kiss into her hair.

She kept herself relaxed, despite the sudden clench in her gut.

She hated the thought of the end of the week.

"It will just be a couple of hours," she finally murmured. "I don't want you to neglect your sister."

He tilted her head up toward him, searching her face for a few moments. Then he kissed her on the mouth and got out of bed. "I'm going to take a shower. You can think about how you'd like to spend the day while I'm gone."

She smiled at him. "Good plan."

Cyrus got up and went into the bathroom. She heard the shower turn on, and she stretched out under the covers, enjoying the aftermath of her orgasms and the lazy thrill of lying in bed in the morning without having any particular reason to get up.

She wasn't—*wasn't*—going to think about the end of their week together, coming up very soon now.

When the shower turned off, though, she managed to pull her gown over her head again and then heave herself out of the bed. She kind of had to pee, and a shower would be nice.

She padded over to the mirror above the dresser and actually gave a little shriek at what she saw.

Cyrus stuck his head out of the bathroom. "What's the matter?"

"Why didn't you tell me my hair looked this bad?" she demanded, horrified by the image in the mirror. Her cheeks were bright red, and she had a sheen of perspiration on her skin. Her breasts looked a little too jiggly without the support of a bra. But all that wasn't too bad, just the natural result of sex and being undressed.

But her hair. *Her hair.*

She'd gone to bed with it still damp, always a bad idea. It had snarled and kinked during the night so it stuck out all over in unattractive flips, waves, and tangles. She was mortified to think she'd just had sex with Cyrus looking like this.

"What?" he said, his lips twitching in a familiar way. "I thought it looked nice."

She tried to huff, but it came out as more of a squeak. She'd felt so sexy earlier. And the way he'd been looking at her had made her feel almost beautiful. But she'd actually looked like *this*. "That's what you were laughing at when you first saw me this morning!"

"Certainly not."

"Liar!" She whimpered a little and tried to smooth her tangles down. Her hands did absolutely no good. "I knew you were laughing at me. Why didn't you tell me?"

Cyrus laughed and came out of the bathroom with a towel wrapped around his waist. He slid an arm around her from behind and leaned over to nuzzle her hair. "Sexiest thing I've ever seen. Why would I laugh at that?"

She didn't believe him, but she felt a little bit better.

~

The following day, late in the afternoon, Brie sat with Cyrus on a bench on Tybee Island, looking out into the ocean.

The past two days had been wonderful. The day before, they'd explored Savannah, discovering a couple of small, historic churches that neither of them had seen before. Then today they'd driven out to Tybee Island and had a lovely time walking around and eating seafood. They'd had sex again last night in Cyrus's bed—slow and tender and gentle, lasting longer than Brie had even known lovemaking could last. They hadn't this morning, but the time they'd spent together had meant a lot more to her than a weekend of non-stop sex ever could have.

But they were nearing the end of Sunday afternoon. And Cyrus was leaving town tomorrow.

The week was just about over.

Despite her constant reminders that this time was only temporary, she still wanted to cry at the thought.

Cyrus hadn't said a word for twenty minutes, and she wondered if he felt the way she did—sad and kind of heavy in the belly. She'd been leaning against him, her cheek resting on the side of his chest, but she lifted her head to check his expression.

He looked quiet and grave. When he met her eyes, she saw a matching emotion.

He didn't want the week to end either.

Just then, they were both distracted by a voice approaching them. A hassled woman had a little boy tightly by the hand and was half dragging him toward the bench beside them. "Since you can't seem to behave," the woman said in an exasperated voice, "and you don't want to be nice to your sisters, you can sit on a bench by yourself and sulk."

The boy's face was mulish as he sat down hard. Brie saw what must be his family sitting on a blanket nearby, happily looking at maps and brochures.

"Poor little fellow," Brie whispered. "He probably thinks Savannah is a terrible place to spend his vacation."

Cyrus's eyes had been resting on the boy—who looked lonely and miserable. But at her words, he murmured, "Yes. I'm not sure a boy his age would know how to appreciate it."

"Not like we do." Her words returned them to their previous, slightly poignant mood. She gave Cyrus an ironic half smile. "It's already Sunday."

"I know." His arm around her shoulders tightened a little, and he stared blankly out at the ocean.

They'd only had a week. They'd both known that going into this. Brie was not going to complain or feel sorry for herself. She doubted Cyrus would have let her get as close to him as he had if there had been any possibility of a future.

Then Cyrus blurted out, "Maybe we should change our terms."

She gasped, a flicker of hope she'd never allowed coming alive in her heart.

Maybe he felt the way she did. Maybe he was starting to think that there was too much potential between them to let it end after just a week.

Maybe he wanted a real relationship—the way she had to admit she did.

Maybe it wasn't as impossible as she'd believed.

"What terms?" she asked breathlessly, straightening up so she could look at him.

He looked momentarily uncomfortable, as if he couldn't believe he'd just said what he'd said. But then he explained, "Christmas isn't for another week. I don't actually have to leave Savannah quite yet." He cleared his throat. "What if I stay in town a few more days? Would you... would you be amenable to that idea?"

Her racing heart dropped painfully.

He didn't want a relationship. He just wanted to make the week a little bit longer.

Had he suggested such a thing even that morning, she would have said yes without hesitation. She would love to have a few more days with him.

But her reaction just now really scared her. If she was so far gone right now—so desperately wanting more from him, despite her attempts not to—then how would she feel a few days from now when they still would have to say good-bye.

Cyrus must have read her expression and her hesitation. "You don't want me to stay," he murmured.

Her eyes shot up to his face, and she saw disappointment and something like pain there. She'd hurt him. She hated the idea of it.

But this was getting more and more dangerous for her.

"I *do* want you to stay," she said, her tone slightly wobbly from the confusion of her feelings. "I would love to spend a few more days with you. I'm just... I'm just wondering if it's wise."

She used his words from the day last week when they'd discussed their original terms since they were the only ones she could come up with.

He let out a breath and looked out toward the ocean. "It's not wise. Of course it's not."

"I'm not saying no," she said, leaning against him again. "I just... don't know."

"Think about it," Cyrus said mildly after a long moment. "You can tell me this evening."

Brie's eyes darted over to his face, and she knew she'd hurt his feelings by not responding to his offer with enthusiasm. She felt guilty and confused and tempted and torn and absolutely terrified. "Okay," she managed to say. "I'll think about it."

Then, when she couldn't stand the awkwardness, she added, "I'm going over to that tourist shop behind us and buy some trinkets for Christmas gifts. I'll be back in ten or fifteen minutes."

Cyrus nodded. "I'll be here." He didn't offer to join her. He obviously knew she was trying to get away for a little while.

She hurried toward the shop, which was in the strip of stores farther up toward the street. She glanced back at Cyrus before she entered and could only see him from behind. But even his shoulders and the back of his head looked stiff and tense.

With a twisting of her gut, she made herself turn away. She went into the store and stood staring at T-shirts and mugs. But after two minutes, she let out a thick sigh and started back to Cyrus.

She shouldn't have run away. She still didn't know what to do, but leaving him wasn't the way to find out answers.

Brie had expected to find him stewing over her desertion, so she halted in surprise when she saw he was talking to the boy on the bench next to his.

He hadn't seen her since she was behind him. Intrigued, Brie approached quietly so she could hear what they were discussing.

"It's dumb," the little boy said. "I'm sick of boring nature and stupid old buildings. We can't even really go to the beach and get in the water because my mom says it too *cold*."

"There are a lot of old buildings around here, aren't there?" Cyrus said, his voice mild and casual. "Can't blame you for getting tired of them."

"I wanted to go to Disney World," the boy said, glaring over at the rest of his family.

"What did you want to do there?"

Brie felt oddly touched at hearing this conversation between sophisticated, guarded Cyrus and a sulky little boy. Still shamelessly eavesdropping, she waited to hear what they would say next.

"I wanted to go on a new ride that has sword fighting and everything." The boy swung his arm back and forth as if he were trying to fence with an invisible sword. "Greg, my friend, said it was so cool. He got to go during the summer."

"And you came here instead," Cyrus said, a sympathetic note in his voice. "There was a lot of fighting here too," he added almost indifferently. "A long time ago."

The boy gave him a suspicious look. "What do you mean fighting?"

"When the Union armies came through and laid siege to Fort Pulaski, over that way. Then later they burned down a lot of the old buildings."

The boy blinked at this blunt statement, but his lips parted slightly with interest. "They burned down the stupid old buildings?"

Cyrus nodded sagely. "That's what armies do."

"What kind of armies?"

Cyrus started to tell the boy about the siege of Fort Pulaski and Savannah. He had an impressive knowledge of the history, and he informed the boy of numbers, weapons, and a number of rather gruesome incidents that made even Brie raise her eyebrows.

The boy's eyes grew wider and wider with growing interest, and he finally said, "Wow."

"When you leave here, be sure to look for Fort Pulaski."

Brie looked at the boy's face. It was no longer remotely sulky. Then she looked back at Cyrus's profile. His expression was bland and matter-of-fact, but she had the ridiculous urge to cover his face with kisses.

She put her hand on her breastbone, on a little clench there that had started to ache. And she understood something. Despite her fear, despite the inevitable risk to her heart, she was going to agree to his new terms.

Because there was no way she'd be able to let Cyrus leave tomorrow morning.

~

When they got back to the house, Brie had to go to the bathroom.

The trip back had been quiet. Not awkward exactly but quiet and almost tired. Brie hadn't known exactly how to tell Cyrus she wanted to extend their time a few more days, and he'd made a point of changing the subject when she rejoined him on the bench. So when they returned from their trip to Tybee Island, Cyrus still didn't know she'd made up her mind.

She went to find him after she finished in the bathroom, realizing it was silly not to let him know her decision—merely because she was a little embarrassed at having come to the conclusion so quickly, so surely, as she'd watched him talk to the boy.

Hearing voices down the hall, she followed them to Cyrus's office.

"Do I need to arrange for the car tomorrow morning?" Gordon was asking.

There was a pause from the office, where Cyrus stood beyond the range of her vision. "I don't know."

"You haven't yet offered her an alternative?"

Brie almost smiled at the mild disapproval in Gordon's voice—as if he was discreetly chiding his employer for not stepping up the way he was expected to.

The knowledge that Cyrus had stepped up, that he'd blurted out the idea of his staying longer so sincerely, pushed Brie into action.

Seeing her approach, Gordon stepped out of the way so Brie could enter the office. "No need for the car tomorrow morning," she said softly. She saw Cyrus's expression change as she approached him. "I'd like you to stay a little longer if you still want to."

A little spark alit in Cyrus's eyes, although his face remained composed. "You're sure?"

Brie nodded. "I've got nothing to do until Christmas anyway."

"Very good," Gordon murmured. He appeared to be hiding a smile. "I will arrange for dinner tonight. Around seven?"

"Yes. Thank you." Cyrus's eyes hadn't left Brie's.

When Gordon had left the room, Cyrus pulled her closer to him, draping his arms around her waist. "How long do you want me to stay?"

She assumed he'd be rather flabbergasted if she told him the truth—that she wanted him to never leave. So she just smiled and said, "As long as you can."

His brows drew together. "I can stay until Friday. Then I really need to join my nephew and his family."

"Then Friday it is."

~

The next morning, Cyrus woke up with his right arm nearly numb and something hot and heavy pressing into his chest.

His crisis instincts automatically triggered, he jerked his eyes open, on guard and ready to face a possible threat.

He let out his breath as soon as he oriented himself.

His first fully conscious thought was to wonder how it could possibly be comfortable for Brie to sleep smashed up against his side like this, with her upper body resting on his chest. He certainly wasn't very comfortable. The arm he was using to hold her against him was prickling from lack of circulation. He was painfully stiff from having her weight trap him in place for so long. And he was way too hot, her little sleeping body generating heat like a radiator.

He needed to adjust—to give himself some space, to stretch his stiff limbs, to renew blood flow to his arm.

But Cyrus didn't move, except to use his free hand to gently stroke Brie's hair, which was spilling all over both of them.

After they'd had sex the evening before, he'd gone to sleep with Brie curled up against him in this position. He couldn't believe neither one of them had rolled away during the night. He'd never had the urge to hold someone like this before.

Brie's cheek was pressed against his bare chest, and the spot where their skin connected seemed to burn. Her steady breathing raised and lowered her back slightly, and her hands instinctively curled around his shoulder and side. Her loose hair was tousled and beautiful, cloaking them like a blanket.

He really was very uncomfortable. But it was Monday now, and he only had four more mornings to hold her this way.

It was troubling—this urge to hold her. As troubling as his desire for sex with her so often, which had genuinely surprised him with its continued power since he was well past that stage in his life.

He'd thought he was anyway.

Friday. He'd given himself until Friday to enjoy her, to indulge in the kind of pleasure and companionship that was otherwise impossible in his life. To get her out of his system.

He was afraid it wasn't working.

The realization finally prompted him to move from his position in bed. He gently tried to extricate himself from her sprawled body on top of him, but she clung tenaciously in her sleep, her unconscious self insistent on cuddling. He tried to roll her over, but his numb arm was still trapped beneath her. And before he could free it, she just rolled back and snuggled up against him once more.

She mumbled incoherently as he eased her body up to retrieve his arm. He did so successfully but only to find that Brie had contentedly curled up farther down his body with her head resting on his belly.

Cyrus shook out his numb arm, chuckling softly over the absurdity of his dilemma. But when he felt tenderness swell up in his chest from the sight of Brie sleeping on his stomach, he shook his head silently and rolled his body away.

Brie made a wordless grumble and groped out for him again.

"Sorry," he murmured, gently pulling her up so her head was on her pillow. "I have to get up."

She was barely awake. She mumbled something like "M'okee" and folded up in a little ball.

Cyrus left her to walk into the bathroom. He adjusted the water temperature in the shower less hot than normal, trying to cool himself down and jolt himself out of his groggy softness.

When he got out and dried off, he brushed his teeth. He stared down at Brie's toothbrush right next to his. Her hairbrush lay next to the sink with her makeup bag and a few bottles of lotions and creams. Since they'd decided to extend their time together, she'd gone home yesterday evening to get an overnight bag with some things she would need.

He stood in his bathroom with his toothbrush in his mouth and tried to process how he felt about it.

It was an invasion of his privacy, a raid on his personal space, a disturbingly intimate blow to the comfortable, isolated lifestyle he'd maintained for so long.

And he liked it.

He liked the sight of her toothbrush next to his, Brie sleeping in his bed.

It was an absurd, irrational response. He knew better. He'd been lonely a long time, so perhaps that explained it. He'd cling to anyone, anything, who could help fill the void.

But he'd never wanted any other woman around all the time, even back when he'd had a social life.

He'd been acquainted with Brie for only eight days, and they had no future. His life was in England. Hers was here. Both of them understood that this was just temporary. It was the only reason Cyrus had been able to let himself go the way he had. Had there been a possibility of a future, he never would have taken so many risks.

He wasn't foolish enough to overlook the way he was becoming attached to her. He knew it would be hard when he left. He knew he'd need some time to get over her absence in his life. It would be worth it though. He felt alive again.

It had been so long since he felt that way.

When he heard the phone ring and saw it was Benjamin, he reached to pick it up. It was early, and his nephew didn't normally call at this time.

Benjamin was calling with an invitation to join him and his mother for a visit to the cemetery. Lucy's oldest son Michael, Benjamin's brother, was buried there.

Cyrus felt his heart drop. He didn't want to go to the cemetery to visit his nephew's grave. It made him think of a host of things he didn't want to think about. He'd rather stay in his bubble with Brie and not let the rest of the world in.

But he accepted the invitation anyway. He didn't believe in indulging himself at the cost of his family.

He got dressed quickly and told Gordon to let Brie know he'd be back before nine. Then he drove out to the cemetery, where he found Lucy waiting, standing next to Benjamin and his wife Mandy, with their infant son in her arms.

Benjamin had gotten a job in an architecture firm in Savannah a few months ago, so the family had moved here from California. Cyrus knew Lucy was thrilled to have her son and grandson so much closer.

Cyrus felt a pain in his chest at the sight of them, and it didn't go away as they walked slowly over to Michael's grave.

They didn't stay for very long. Lucy put flowers on the grave, and they stood around, sharing a few thoughts or memories. Lucy teared up, but she didn't really cry, and Mandy kept reaching out to touch Benjamin's back as if in support.

Benjamin had grown his beard back, although it wasn't as long and straggly as it used to be. He was a big man with dark eyes and a gruff voice, but Cyrus knew emotions ran deep in him.

Benjamin had gone years without talking to his extended family. Because of him. Because of Cyrus.

The pain in Cyrus's chest intensified.

He couldn't help but wonder what Brie would think if she knew how he'd behaved with Michael, with Benjamin, with all his nephews at one point or another.

He'd told her that he'd been a dictator, but she hadn't seemed to really believe it.

She would believe it. If she ever knew who he was for real. She'd believe it, and that soft, admiring look in her eyes would be gone for good.

After about a half hour, they started to leave. Lucy gave him a hug. Then Mandy did. Then Benjamin did.

Cyrus returned all their hugs, but he felt a resistance rising inside him, an armor he'd always used when life hurt him too much. He needed to get away from them. He needed to be alone.

He sat in his car and pretended to work on his phone until the others had driven away. Then he got back out and walked to Michael's grave again, standing stiffly and staring down at the gray, chiseled stone marker.

Starting in high school, Michael and Benjamin had spent their summers working for Cyrus in England. Lucy had thought it was a great opportunity for the boys, and back then Cyrus had been hoping that all five of his nephews would be part of Damon Enterprises eventually.

As it turned out, only Harrison had wanted it.

But it was during one of those summers that Michael had died in a car accident. Another victim of the Damon curse, the papers had said. Tragedy followed tragedy. Michael wasn't the only one to die in the accident. A girl with him in the car had died as well—the sister of Marietta, Harrison's wife. And Marietta herself had been terribly injured.

They'd found out years later—far too late—that Michael had been drunk.

All of it was Cyrus's fault. Michael had been a wild, foolish boy, but he'd been rebelling against Cyrus. Just as Benjamin had been rebelling when he cut himself off from his family for years.

Cyrus was the one who had pushed the boys into rebellion with his impossibly high standards and his ruthless pressure.

He'd thought he'd been doing what was best for them—using his influence to make them into good, strong men. But he'd only succeeded in pushing them away, pushing them into bad decisions.

He didn't want Brie to know. Ever.

He didn't want her to ever look at him with knowledge in her eyes, with disappointment, with disillusionment. She thought he was good and giving and worthy.

He wasn't.

He stood over the grave, not moving a muscle until after nine o'clock. He glanced down at his watch and knew Brie was expecting him back at the house. She would have woken up by now. Gordon would have told her he was returning soon.

Cyrus didn't move. He kept staring down at Michael's grave, his chest hurting so much it was clouding his brain.

When Harrison had fallen in love with Marietta and they'd found out the truth about the car accident that had killed Michael and her sister, Cyrus had done everything possible to put an end to the relationship. He'd seen how much they loved each other, and yet he'd thought they'd be better off apart anyway.

He'd almost destroyed Harrison, whom he loved like a son.

That was evidently what he always did to the people he loved.

At ten o'clock, his body was aching from standing motionless for so long. He was too old to do this sort of thing. He needed to sit down, relax, walk off the stiffness.

Instead, he called Gordon.

"How are you, sir?" Gordon asked. "Are you on your way back?"

Cyrus didn't answer the first question. "No."

Gordon paused. "Miss Brie has been waiting for you."

Cyrus felt physically ill. He could picture her waiting—hope and trust and laughter and deep empathy in her eyes. "I think it's probably best if you tell her to go home."

There was an even longer pause before Gordon answered. "She will be... confused. I told her to expect you by nine, as you said."

It felt like ages since that morning, when he'd thought he'd just be gone an hour or two and would return to spend another day with Brie. "I know. Tell her plans changed."

"When will you be back, sir?"

"I don't know." He hung up then because Gordon was making him feel guilty and weak.

He needed to move, to walk, to stretch, but he didn't. His back hurt intensely, but he almost welcomed the pain.

He was Cyrus Damon. He'd never been anyone else. And Cyrus Damon had forged his place in the world a long time ago.

The universe didn't allow do-overs. You paid the price for the decisions you'd made, and wanting a different future didn't mean you could actually get one.

Of all people, Cyrus didn't deserve one.

He didn't even deserve the last few days he had remaining with Brie.

He stood at Michael's grave until after noon, until his back and legs had clenched up so badly he could no longer stay on his feet. He went back to his car then because he physically had to sit down, but he still didn't drive home.

He didn't want to return to the house to find Brie gone.

He didn't want to return to the house at all.

Finally he had no choice. His head was pounding, he was weak from going without food and water all day, and he couldn't seem to straighten up his back. He managed to drive home, shocked when he saw Brie's car was still in the driveway.

He just sat behind the wheel, staring at it in a pained daze.

After a few minutes—he had no idea how many—someone was opening his driver's side door. It was Brie, he realized, reaching down to pull him out of the car.

"Oh my God, Cyrus," she was murmuring hoarsely, helping him to stand up. "What happened? What's wrong?"

There was absolutely no way for him to explain.

He still couldn't stand fully upright because of the clench in his back, but he managed to limp into the house with Brie at his side.

Trying to sound like his normal self, he saw Gordon waiting in the entryway and said, "I'm fine. I just need some coffee."

"Not coffee," Brie said, turning his face so she could look at it. "You don't need caffeine right now." She looked over at Gordon. "Maybe some water first."

Cyrus tried to object to this overruling of his wishes, but he simply didn't have the focus or energy.

"What's wrong with your back?" Brie asked gently.

"I was standing in one place too long. I can just walk it off."

"You don't look like you could walk very far. You need to lie down. Oh wait, I know. You should get in the hot tub. That will definitely help."

"I don't care for hot tubs."

"I don't care what you care for. You look terrible, so you need to do it anyway."

Cyrus wasn't going to have this. He deserved to be in pain, and he certainly wasn't used to anyone bossing him around, making him do things he didn't want to do. He needed to put Brie in her place even if it meant hurting her feelings.

He opened his mouth to do just that. No sound came out.

"Here's the water," Brie said, taking the glass from Gordon's hand as he approached. "Now drink this and don't be ridiculous."

So despite his intentions, he ended up drinking the water. Then he ended up soaking in the hot tub, which felt so good on his painfully tense muscles that he kept having to stifle embarrassing moans.

When he'd drank two glasses of water, Brie handed him a glass of white wine instead, taking one for herself as she climbed into the hot tub beside him.

Cyrus closed his eyes, feeling better but trying to remember all the resolutions he'd come to that morning about Brie.

He couldn't have her. No matter how much he wanted her, he couldn't have her.

Brie stretched out a hand to gently rub his sore neck. "Do you want to tell me what happened this morning?"

He didn't want to tell her. He couldn't tell her. It would reveal far too much about his real self, the self he didn't want her to see.

She was massaging the tight muscles just at the nape of his neck. "Gordon said you went to a cemetery?"

And that was enough. His mind clouded with the release of tension and a warm relaxation from the water and the wine, Cyrus started to tell her. He avoided as many details as possible that might give away his identity, but he told her about the accident, about Michael dying, about the ways he'd pushed his nephew into rebellion, into tragedy.

He rambled on and on. He never talked so much. He certainly never opened up this way—with anyone.

He just couldn't seem to help it at the moment, like the last cord holding back his will had snapped.

Brie listened quietly, occasionally asking a question. She didn't pull away. She kept rubbing his neck, his shoulder, the back of his head, as if she were trying to caress away his tension.

Finally, he'd told her everything—laid himself out for her to judge, for her to hate, for her to walk away from.

She tilted her head down to nuzzle his shoulder. "Oh my God, Cyrus! How could you possibly think all that was your fault?"

"Didn't you hear me?"

"Of course I did. You made some mistakes. Everyone makes mistakes. You're not responsible for the decisions of other people. And you're certainly not responsible for car crashes when you weren't behind the wheel."

"I just told you—"

"I know what you told me. I get why you feel guilty. It's totally natural. I'm just telling you there's nothing real underlying the guilt. So standing in one place for hours today until you were about to fall over just to punish yourself is completely irrational." She eased close enough to press a soft kiss on his jaw. "I think you know it too."

For the first time, a flicker of insight and irony pierced through the bleak daze of his mind, letting him see himself as if from outside, letting him realize how foolish he'd been acting. He looked her in the eyes, seeing her expression softening with what might have been relief.

She smiled at him. "How's your back?"

"It's better."

"Good. Let's get out. I'm kind of hungry. I haven't had much to eat today, and I know you haven't had anything."

So they got out, showered, changed into comfortable clothes, and went into the lounge to eat a very late lunch or a very early dinner. They drank more wine, and afterward Cyrus was feeling so much better, so relaxed and exhausted, that he could barely sit up straight.

Somehow—he had no idea how it happened—he ended up sprawled on the big couch with his head in Brie's lap. She was stroking his hair and his face with a tenderness that made his heart ache.

He wondered faintly if she was putting pieces of his identity together but then realized she was so young that she probably hadn't been old enough to follow the news when Michael's accident happened.

She was so much younger than him. He shouldn't be letting her do this to him, shouldn't be letting her make him feel so good.

He could barely keep his eyes opened.

"Why did you stay?" he mumbled, unable to hold back the question.

"Because I knew something was wrong. You're far too much of a gentleman to send me away like that if something hadn't been seriously wrong. And Gordon looked worried. I wasn't going to leave if something was wrong with you."

"I'm glad you stayed." He shouldn't be saying that. He absolutely shouldn't be saying that. He really needed to start holding her at arm's length so he'd be able to walk away from her at the end of the week.

He didn't have any other choice.

It felt like she was smiling above him, but his eyes were closed so he couldn't see her.

~

When he woke up, Brie was stretched out beside him on the couch, and he was holding her in his arms.

He lifted his head and saw that it was after seven in the evening.

Brie had been asleep too, but his motion must have woken her because she shifted against him and opened her eyes. "How are you?" she asked groggily.

"I'm fine. I'm good. How about you?"

"I'm great. I haven't had a nap like that in ages."

"Me either."

"You still look tired." Her eyes were gently scanning his face.

He was. The morning had completely leveled him, and he felt like he could sleep for another ten hours. He just gave her a little smile and kissed her.

For a long time they just kissed, slowly sliding their lips and their tongues against each other. He loved the feel of her against him like this, slow and mild and not at all urgent. His body responded to her closeness though—not intensely but enough to make him harden about halfway. He was afraid he wasn't up for sex. He wasn't sure he had the energy or focus to manage intercourse at the moment.

If Brie wanted it, however, he would figure out some way to give it to her.

They were still kissing when he felt her hand sliding beneath his waistband until she was stroking and holding his half erection.

"Brie," he rasped, trying to get his mind to work, his body to work, this languid spell that had come over him to disperse.

"Shh." She kissed him again, smiling against his lips and stroking his head with her free hand. Her other hand kept pumping his erection, holding it up against his lower belly as he hardened a little more.

Her lips clung to his, and she remained in his embrace. Her hand was firm and skillful as she worked him up to climax before he was ever fully hard. Cyrus felt his muscles tightening and a familiar coil of pressure. He kept giving Brie clumsy, unfocused kisses all the while.

It took only a minute, after the pleasure had faded, for his breathing to even out again. Brie grabbed a tissue to clean up his come, and Cyrus let his body soften with a kind of relaxation he rarely experienced.

He opened his mouth to suggest a way of pleasing her now, but Brie spoke before he could. "Don't you dare suggest something silly. You need to sleep. That's all I wanted to do."

His eyes were already closing again. He was never like this. Hopefully tomorrow he'd be more himself again. "Thank you. Take care of... tomorrow."

He knew—without doubt—that if Brie hadn't been here, he wouldn't have gone to sleep tonight at all. He would have stayed awake, mentally torturing himself all night. And he never would have felt this good.

He couldn't remember ever feeling this good.

He'd never felt cared for like this. Not once in his life.

As Brie got up to go to the bathroom, Cyrus wondered in a wave a vague dismay how he would ever survive after they parted ways on Friday.

Only a few more days. Then he'd have to remember what it felt like to live his life alone.

Six

On Thursday morning, Cyrus sat with Brie at a bench in one of the squares off Bull Street.

They'd gotten up early so they could wander the streets during the quietest part of the day, before tourists started to swarm the shops and sidewalks. The day was clear and brisk, and there was a nip to the air that hadn't been there earlier this week. The shops and streetlights were all decorated for the holidays, but it still didn't feel like Christmas to Cyrus. It was too warm. Not nearly festive enough.

It felt more like the end of summer as they sipped the last of their bottled water and sat in soft silence, watching the city come to life.

Cyrus's arm was draped around Brie, pulling her snugly against his side. She leaned against him, occasionally stroking his chest in a fond, idle way that made him ache behind his ribs.

Cyrus had been to this city many times before. His sister had lived here since she'd gotten married. But he'd never breathed in the city like this before, and he knew he'd never be able to come here again without thinking about Brie.

Tomorrow was Friday.

Tomorrow he'd have to leave her for good.

Almost unconsciously, he lifted his hand to brush along her long, soft hair, burnished now by the sunshine

Cyrus had a crazy, passing thought. He wondered what she would say if he blurted out a proposal—if he asked her to marry him. Right here. Right now.

He wanted to ask her.

He wasn't so foolish as to do it though.

He'd known her for less than two weeks. He was far too old for her. And he could hardly burden her with everything that came along with being Cyrus Damon. Even with all he'd poured out to her in the hot tub earlier that week, she would have no idea of the baggage he brought with him.

Plus Brie would never say yes.

"It's a golden sort of morning, isn't it?" Brie's voice broke the stillness. It was soft, strangely resigned.

"Yes. It is." He knew she meant the sunlight, which was streaming in through the bare trees, burnishing everything it touched with an almost overpowering gold. Summer or winter, Savannah could still offer them *this*.

"Life sometimes sucks, doesn't it?"

"Yes." Intuitively he understood that her thoughts had followed the same paths as his over the past few minutes.

"I guess there's no way to stretch out today any longer—I mean, make it last for a few more months."

He let out a long breath, oddly touched by the hesitant, half-teasing statement. "I think that's more than I'm capable of doing."

"Yeah," she said, raising a hand to cup his cheek briefly. "I know."

He nodded to let her know he understood, but he couldn't think of anything to say.

"It's just that two weeks doesn't seem long enough," she continued, slouching against his side again and staring out at the drooping oaks. "I mean, it seems like we have something good here, and it's too bad that this is all it can be."

She'd voiced his own feelings so perfectly that there was nothing he could add.

"Not that I'm assuming it was serious," she added hurriedly, evidently misunderstanding his silence. "I mean, we both knew it was temporary going into this. I've just had such a good time."

"Me too," he said softly. "I know what you mean."

She paused. Then took a shuddering breath and asked very softly, "I guess... I guess keeping in touch is... is out of the question?"

His breath hitched at the tentative question. He knew exactly what the question meant. She was sending out a little test balloon to see how he'd react.

To see if he was at all open to extending their relationship.

It hurt. So much. That he'd have to kill the slightest bit of hope he could hear in her voice. "I don't think there would be any good in doing that," he murmured gently.

He felt her slump against him, wounded that he'd had to wound her.

But there was no way. Absolutely no way. He'd been someone else these past two weeks—someone different, someone just for her. But that person couldn't last—not when he had to go back home and be who he'd always been.

If he'd had a minor breakdown on Monday at being so close to her, it would only get worse if he really considered a life with her.

"Okay," she said rather hoarsely.

He kissed her hair. "I'm sorry, dear heart. But it would never work."

"I understand."

He doubted she did understand, but there was no way for him to make it clearer—not without sharing with her exactly who he was and everything that came with it.

He'd known—he'd *known*—they had no future. He'd made conscious choices when he'd agreed to spend the week with her and then a few more days beyond that. He was an intelligent adult who knew how to weigh options. And now he could live with the consequences.

He just hadn't realized twelve days ago how completely Brie would disarrange his whole world.

"It's just bad timing," Brie concluded, obviously taking some comfort in finally articulating what both of them had clearly been brooding over. "Really bad timing. Just one of those things. I'm going to miss you like hell when you leave." She slanted a shy look up at his face at this confession. "But I still don't regret this time we've had together. Do you?"

"Never." To his embarrassment, he heard his voice crack a little, so he kept his response to one word. But he tightened his arm around her, determined to enjoy the time they had left and not dwell on the misery that would wait for him when he left.

"Never," she repeated in a whisper.

They didn't speak again. Didn't need to. After a few minutes, Cyrus couldn't hold back the need to kiss her. So he rearranged her body and found her lips in a slow, thorough kiss.

She kissed him back immediately, opening her mouth to his advances and gently caressing his hair, his head. The embrace was more tender than erotic, and it went on for a long time.

He didn't know how long they would have kissed—on a public park bench in the most popular part of Savannah—had they not been interrupted by a rowdy group of tourists. A couple of the young guys hooted at them playfully.

Brie giggled as she pulled away from him, rubbing her rosy mouth self-consciously. "I guess we should probably stop."

"Yes," Cyrus agreed, heaving himself to his feet. He had very little time left to kiss Brie, to touch her, to talk to her, to feel her beside him. "I guess it's time."

~

They spent the day wandering aimlessly and occasionally stopping at cafés to eat or drink coffee. When they got back to the house that evening, they had a quiet dinner, and Brie went to take a bath before bed.

As she soaked in the tub, Brie kept telling herself not to be sad.

She'd had an amazing couple of weeks. She'd told Cyrus the truth when she'd said she didn't regret the time she'd spent with him. But she realized now she'd been holding on to the slightest glimmer of hope—that he'd want to stay in touch, that there might be some potential for a future after all.

She'd been foolish. She'd been wrong. And now she had to live with the disappointment.

She told herself she'd feel better when she went up to Eden Manor and had Christmas with Mitchell and the others. She'd feel more normal then. She wouldn't feel like her heart had been ripped apart and trampled on. But she was seriously considering just going home this evening instead of spending one more night with Cyrus. Since she was going to leave him forever tomorrow anyway, maybe she should just get it over with quickly so it wouldn't hurt so much.

It was going to hurt like hell either way.

She was still trying to decide as she got out of the tub and dried off. When her phone rang, she glanced at it and saw the caller was her mother.

Her first instinct was to let it go to voice mail since she wasn't in the mood for chatting right now. But her mother had already called twice this week, and Brie hadn't taken those calls either. Her mother had raised Brie and Mitchell alone since she hadn't been married to either of their fathers. A few years ago, she'd moved to Florida to live with her sister, so Brie only saw her a few times a year. She didn't want her mother to be worried or hurt by her ignoring her calls.

So she took a deep breath and connected the call. "Hi, Mom."

"Brie, is everything all right?"

"Of course it is. Why wouldn't it be?"

"Mitchell said there's a guy."

Brie managed to smother a groan. "Mitchell had no business telling you that."

"Well, I hadn't been able to reach you, so I called to ask him what was going on. And he said there was a guy, and he thought it might be serious."

"I told him it's not serious. I've told him more than once."

"He doesn't believe you. I guess he's been picking up serious vibes, and he's worried that you won't tell him anything."

Brie sat down on the bed in the master bedroom, the towel wrapped around her. She felt worse than ever, her stomach churning at the thought of Mitchell, her mother, everyone thinking and wondering about what was going on with her. "I told him everything there is to tell. I've been hanging out with someone for the past week or so, but there's... there's no potential for anything long-term." Her mother had never been particularly traditional or conservative, but Brie was still slightly uncomfortable talking openly about sex with her.

"How do you know?"

"We agreed on that from the beginning."

"And did you mean it?"

Brie started to reply automatically, but then the question hit her strangely. "I... I did mean it."

"But you don't now?"

"It doesn't matter. Nothing is going to happen. I'm keeping everything in perspective. I've got this under control."

Her mother actually laughed. "Brie, do you think I don't know you? Since when have you ever been able to keep your heart under control?"

Never. Brie had never been able to keep her heart under control. Never in her life.

And it felt more out of control with Cyrus than it had ever felt before.

"Mom, please," she said, her voice slightly hoarse. "I'm an adult. I know I've done stupid things before and lost my heart over things, over men, that I shouldn't have. But this is different. You don't have to worry about me."

"Is it different?" Her mother paused for a moment before she continued, "Brie, you wouldn't be *you* if you didn't go all in with your heart. Giving your heart isn't wrong. The only mistake you've made in the past was giving it to men who didn't deserve it."

Brie swallowed hard, her emotions so raw after trying to hold them back all day with Cyrus that she just couldn't contain them anymore. "But I don't want to make that mistake again. It… it hurts too much. And this is obviously the wrong man since he doesn't want things to continue."

"How do you know he's not going through exactly what you're going through? If he's really different from those other guys, you're going to be able to tell pretty easily. The problem with Chase and the others is that they cared more about themselves than they did about you. If he cares more about you than he does about himself, then your heart is going to be safe."

Brie sat for a minute, silent and shaking slightly as she processed the words and all the feelings that came with them. Finally she said, "I… I don't know."

"You will, Brie. So you made a few mistakes. Everyone does. You're not as foolish as you think you are. You're going to be able to tell if he's really different."

Despite her emotional state, Brie felt better as she hung up with her mother. She never would have been able to talk like this with Mitchell, but it actually did help to share a little bit with someone who really knew her.

After a minute, she stood up and went to change into a nightgown. She chose a pretty white one that looked slightly vintage that she thought Cyrus would like.

She wasn't going to go home. She was going to stay with him as long as she could.

Her heart was already in this, so it wouldn't do any good going home now. She might as well savor every moment she had with him.

Cyrus wasn't like the other men she'd fallen for in the past.

He was so much better.

~

While Brie was taking a bath, Cyrus had gone downstairs to give his e-mail a quick scan. While he was doing so, Gordon came into the room and stood wordlessly in front of the desk until Cyrus looked up. Since Cyrus had a pretty good idea of what Gordon wanted to say, he was tempted to simply ignore him. But he knew how futile an effort that would be.

Gordon would just stand there—for a full hour if necessary—until Cyrus finally acknowledged him.

"Thank you for dinner tonight," Cyrus said. "Did you need something?"

"I was wondering if there have been any changes to the plans for this weekend."

Cyrus let out a small breath. He'd known he wouldn't be able to escape having this conversation. "No. None."

"You're still heading to Eden Manor tomorrow morning? Alone?"

Cyrus met Gordon's gaze and pondered the irony of feeling so much like he'd let his employee down. "Yes."

"You didn't offer her an alternative?"

Leaning back in his chair, Cyrus felt a twist of annoyance in his chest. He knew Gordon wanted only what was best for him, but the man could be endlessly stubborn. "This was always the plan. What exactly did you expect?"

"There are any number of possibilities," Gordon said mildly, "other than saying good-bye to her for good."

The conversation was making him feel even worse, so Cyrus said in a voice that brooked no opposition, "This was temporary. Both of us are agreed."

It was a sign of Gordon's commitment to his cause that he didn't back down, even given Cyrus's tone of voice. "I am not convinced such an agreement is genuine on both sides. Nor am I convinced it's in either of your best interests."

"Damn it, Gordon," Cyrus snapped, his control breaking because the man was needling so close to the core of pain at his heart. "What do you expect us to do? Elope and live happily ever after?"

"That is one possibility, and it's not as implausible as you imply. But there are other possibilities somewhere in between marriage and never seeing her again. Have you suggested the possibility of keeping in touch, at least just to see what happens?"

"Such a suggestion would be useless."

"I don't understand why it would be useless. You're not letting yourself consider possibilities, and I can't help but think it's because you don't believe you deserve to be—"

"Enough," Cyrus cut in harshly. He'd never seen the quiet man so impassioned, and the implications of Gordon's intensity and the words he was saying threatened to rip Cyrus apart. He couldn't listen.

Gordon didn't say a word in response.

"I'm sorry, Gordon," Cyrus said almost immediately. "I really am."

"I know, sir."

"But certain things are true, and they can never be made untrue. She's young and beautiful and talented and vibrant, and she has a full life waiting for her. She should find a young husband who can give her a family and a long life together. She absolutely does not need to be shackled to a man almost twice her age. A man who would bring with him impossible baggage. A man who has lived most of his life not knowing how to love. I will never do that to her."

Gordon didn't reply, but Cyrus could see he was still arguing in his head.

There was nothing he could do about that though. His mind was made up.

It had been made up from the moment he'd seen a pretty woman with an elusive, cerebral quality that spoke to him, gazing at a painting he loved.

A motion from outside the window distracted him then, and he narrowed his eyes as he peered out into the yard.

It was Brie. She must have gone outside, and she looked as ethereal as a ghost in the moonlight, wearing nothing but a long flimsy white gown.

"What is she doing?" he muttered, straightening up. "It's too cool out there for her this evening."

He left the office and went out the French doors, searching the garden for Brie until he found her in the big cushioned chaise near the fountain. She was pulling a soft blanket up over her.

"What are you doing out here?"

She smiled up at him. "I wanted to see the stars." Then she stretched her arms out toward him, and there was no way he could refuse the invitation.

He got onto the chaise with her, under the blanket. When she leaned up for a kiss, he willingly obliged. The kiss was deep and tender but not particularly urgent. Cyrus was no longer young, and he had plenty of patience and control.

He stroked her thoroughly as his lips and tongue moved sensually against hers. The cool night air added another layer of sensation, and Cyrus hazily wondered why he hadn't been making love in the open air all his life.

He lifted his head so he could look down on her, beautiful and sensuous in the moonlight. His lips parted, but he couldn't say anything, which was just as well. He didn't want anything to spoil the perfect, intimate stillness of the night.

Because he wanted to show Brie exactly how he felt about her, he spent a lot of time kissing and caressing her.

He teased her nipples with his tongue and mouthed his way down to her belly. Her skin tasted slightly of the lavender bath salts she must have just used, and her body was soft and warm and pliant. He loved the sound of her accelerating breathing and how little gasps hitched in her throat whenever he found a spot she particularly liked.

He gently parted her legs to allow room for his head, and then he stroked her open intimately with his tongue.

Her aroused flesh was hot and slightly swollen, and his heart gave a little kick when he inhaled her natural scent. He lapped at her entrance, his groin twitching when she let out a low moan.

Her hands had been fumbling at the cushions, but now she moved them to hold his head in position. He held her open and fluttered his tongue as her body grew more and more tense. Then he closed his lips around her clit and sucked hard.

The tension inside her broke as she let out a sob of pleasure. Her body rode out the spasms of her release, and her fingers clutched at his hair.

He took several deep breaths as her body relaxed and her hand started caressing his head.

"Thank you," she whispered, trying to pull his body up on top of her.

Cyrus responded to her urging and settled his pelvis between her thighs, his mind clearing a little now that he wasn't surrounded by the scent of her arousal. The fragrance of the night and lavender was strong in the air, but it was more manageable than the deep fragrance of how much Brie wanted him.

He kissed her deeply, letting her taste herself in his mouth. Then he found the condom she'd brought with her, rolled it on, and then used his hand to align his erection at her entrance and slowly sank into her body.

Even through the condom, he could vividly feel how wet and hot and tight she was around his erection. He paused for a minute, closing his eyes so she couldn't read the emotion that must be reflected there.

When he felt Brie's hips begin to pump beneath him, he was ready to respond. Their bodies rocked together in a slow, rhythmic motion, and then Cyrus lowered his face for another kiss.

She opened her mouth against his, and his tongue explored her mouth with the same rhythm of his pelvis.

Brie's hands stroked him all over—his head, his back, his thighs, the clenching muscles of his ass. They kissed the whole time, Cyrus only occasionally pulling away so he could bury his face against her neck and soft hair.

It went on a long time, but eventually Brie's little hand explored between his legs until she found his balls. She squeezed them gently, sending shockwaves of pleasure through Cyrus's body.

He grunted, and his body tightened involuntarily.

She kept squeezing, and her motion beneath him grew more urgent. Realizing she was close to coming herself, Cyrus let himself go, pushing inside her with faster, harder strokes.

Soon he felt her clamp down around his erection and her body shake with the tremors of her orgasm. She cried out wordlessly on a taken breath as her body arched beneath his.

At the same time, she gave his balls a hard squeeze. Combined with the pressure of her intimate muscles, the sensations pulled Cyrus into climax himself. He breathed out, "Brie, dear heart!" as the coiled pleasure surged through him.

They lay tangled together on the chaise for a long time as their bodies relaxed, and they continued to kiss and caress each other.

And Cyrus knew this was everything he'd always wanted. All the warmth and tenderness and understanding and kinship he'd been desperately searching for all his life.

He didn't know what he could do about it.

But he knew that, at least for this moment, he was holding everything he'd ever wanted in his arms.

~

They lay in bed as long as they could the next morning. Friday morning. The morning he had to leave.

At about eight thirty, Cyrus went down to get coffee, but then he climbed back into bed with Brie. He was wearing a pair of pajama pants, and she was wearing one of his shirts and nothing else. Her hair was a tangle of kinks and flips, but her cheeks were flushed and her eyes tender and sleepy.

He'd never seen anything more beautiful in his life.

They drank coffee and chatted idly, both of them prolonging the inevitable as long as possible.

He couldn't keep her. Couldn't be selfish. Couldn't saddle her with his conflicted self and all the burdens that came with him—just because he wanted her so much.

He had to let her go.

Gordon came in a half hour later with a breakfast tray and smiled discreetly at Brie's squeal of pleasure over the waffles, bacon, fruit, and cocoa.

Cyrus studied Gordon as the man unloaded the trays, and he noticed a certain expression on his face.

Gordon wasn't displeased with Cyrus anymore, and the reason for the change made Cyrus's heart twist a little.

In his subtle, understated way, Gordon looked satisfied. Pleased. Almost proud.

As if he'd concluded that everything was going to be all right.

It made Cyrus worry. Because he hadn't done what Gordon wanted him to do. He hadn't asked Brie to stay with him forever. He couldn't do that.

He'd told Gordon as much the night before.

But Gordon looked happy anyway, as his eyes rested very briefly on Cyrus and Brie lying together on the bed.

As if Gordon had come to his own conclusions during the night. As if he knew more than his employer did about the outcome of this situation. About Cyrus's future decisions. About just how long he would be able to hold out once Brie had disappeared from his life.

As if he knew more about Cyrus than Cyrus would ever know about himself.

It made Cyrus decidedly nervous.

Gordon didn't look worried at all.

But Cyrus was still going to say good-bye to Brie forever only an hour or two from now.

~

Later that morning, Brie was trying not to cry as Cyrus walked her out to her car.

It was over now. There was no more delaying or pretending. She would never see him again.

Any flicker of hope that had still been burning died completely the day before when she'd talked to Cyrus on the bench. She'd gone as far as she could go in suggesting they leave it open for some sort of a future, and Cyrus had been very clear about it never happening.

So she had no hope left. Just very sweet memories. And aching loss now as she was having to say good-bye to him.

He'd been in a fairly relaxed mood that morning, but he'd grown quieter as the time passed. She knew he wasn't looking forward to their parting, but his face was calm, resigned.

He wasn't, like her, about to cry.

"Gordon put all your belongings in the trunk," Cyrus explained when they reached her car.

"He told me when I said good-bye to him." She was going to miss Gordon too.

She'd been holding Cyrus's hand as they walked, but now she made herself release it. Her palm felt cold and empty.

So did her heart.

"You're leaving later this morning?" she asked, trying to clear the lump in her throat.

"Yes. I need to meet my nephew and his family."

"I hope you have a really good Christmas."

"You too, dear heart." His brown eyes were soft on her face, lingering, like he was caressing her with his look.

Or memorizing her features.

She took a shaky breath. "Thank you. For everything. I mean, the time you spent with me. It... it..." Her throat hurt so much she momentarily couldn't speak, but with another inhale she managed to finish, "I've never been so happy."

He turned his head with a little jerk, staring at a spot in the air for a moment before he met her eyes again and murmured, "Me either."

"Okay." She nodded. Took a breath. Nodded again. "I better go."

He reached up and very gently stroked her face with his knuckles. "Good-bye, Brie. May all your mornings be golden."

And that just about did her in. She had to twist her mouth and close her eyes, but even so a tear slipped out of one eye.

Cyrus brushed it away with his fingertips and didn't say anything else.

She couldn't speak even if she'd known what to say.

She managed to turn away, opening her car door. But she reached back toward him in an instinctive gesture, one she couldn't possibly stop.

He took her hand and squeezed it, and their hands very slowly separated as she made herself get into her car.

She managed not to cry as she pulled her car out onto the road.

She managed not to cry as she looked back and saw Cyrus still standing in the same place, watching her drive away from him.

And she managed not to cry the whole way back to Mitchell's house, which was empty because he and Deanna were already up at Eden Manor. She was going to drive up to meet them there tomorrow.

She unpacked her things from the trunk and found that Cyrus had left something there with her overnight bag and her trinkets in shopping bags.

A wrapped parcel.

She took it inside and carefully unwrapped it to find the painting of the fishing pond that had brought them together in the first place.

He'd bought it for her.

It was only then that she started to cry.

~

The next day, she drove a few hours north to the hilly northern part of the state. There were low, gentle mountains and small quaint towns and lovely lakes surprising her when she rounded turns. Usually she would have enjoyed the drive, but it was hard not to feel bleak and depressed.

Under normal circumstances, she would have enjoyed a Christmas at a Victorian bed and breakfast. Deanna's youngest sister, Kelly, and her husband, Peter, had bought and restored it, and now they ran it, evidently quite successfully for having just opened earlier in the year. She loved Mitchell and Deanna, and she loved Deanna's family, all of whom would be there. Even her crazy, intimidating grandmother.

There would be some other people there as well. Kelly and Peter's investor and his family, she seemed to recall. She hadn't paid much attention to the plans since other things had been occupying her mind.

It was sure to be a beautiful Christmas, but Brie didn't really feel like being social, particularly around people she didn't know.

She couldn't stop thinking about Cyrus.

She arrived midafternoon at the lovely sprawling Victorian house, complete with lake, walled garden, and several different outbuildings. She felt a low stirring of interest, but she had to fight her first thought, which was that Cyrus would love this place too.

She was surprised to see Mitchell coming out the front door and heading down the porch steps and toward her car.

He gave her a hug before she'd barely made it to her feet.

"What was that for?" she asked after returning the hug. She looked up at him and saw concern on his face.

"Nothing," he said. "Just thought you could use it."

Ridiculously her eyes burned for a moment, but she managed to control the emotion. "I could. Thank you." She hadn't told him any details about what had happened with Cyrus, but he'd known there was a guy and that she'd spent more than a week with him.

And he knew it was over now.

He looked at her for a few more moments. "So the thing with that guy wasn't quite as free and easy as you were hoping?"

She took a deep breath. "Not quite. But I'm okay. I don't regret anything."

"Good." He gave her shoulders another squeeze before he got her overnight bag out of her trunk. "Deanna keeps saying I need to give you space and that I'm not to nag you about anything that happened."

Brie couldn't help but chuckle. "That's really good advice."

Mitchell scowled. "That's what I was afraid of."

Despite herself, she felt a little better as she walked with her brother into the house. She stopped in the entryway at the sight of the stained glass windows that framed the front door.

"My God! Are these original?"

"They've been restored by a local craftsman," a voice came from behind her. It was a pleasant male voice, mostly American but with just a trace of a British accent.

She turned to see a very handsome man descending the stairs.

"This is Harrison Damon," Mitchell said. "He invested in this property when Peter and Kelly decided to take it over. This is my sister, Brie."

Brie smiled at the approaching man, thinking he was perhaps the most handsome man she'd ever seen, other than her brother. And also thinking his chocolate-brown eyes were a lot like Cyrus's.

A lot like Cyrus's.

Then she pushed the thought away, determined not to let every random detail she encountered make her think of Cyrus.

"It's very nice to meet you," Harrison said, taking her hand with an intentional courtesy that she really liked.

That courtesy also reminded her of Cyrus, but she wasn't supposed to keep thinking about that.

"You too. So who was the local artisan?" she asked, turning back to the beautiful stained glass panes. "He or she must be a master."

"He is," Harrison said. "His name is Silas Vance. He lives nearby. Perhaps you could meet him while you're here. I believe he's supposed to come to the party tonight."

"I would love that. I work with stained glass."

"Do you? Then you should definitely meet him."

Mitchell switched her bag from one hand to the other and gave her a familiar, teasing look. "I'll take your stuff to your room. You're just at the top of the stairs. Grandmama

Beaufort is in the parlor, presiding over tea with most of the group. You could go in and say hello if you want."

Brie tried not to gulp.

"Or you could have some hot cider," Harrison suggested, evidently reading her expression correctly. "My wife, son, and uncle are in the kitchen. My wife would love to meet you."

"That sounds wonderful," Brie said gratefully. "Maybe I'll start with that."

"You'll have to face Grandmama eventually," Mitchell said in a rather sing-songy voice she knew well from their childhood. "All of us do."

She gave him a cool glare and then followed Harrison to the left, the opposite side of the house from the parlor.

They walked into the kitchen—which had clearly been recently renovated with commercial-grade appliances—and Brie was already fixing her smile for the pretty, sunny-faced blonde who looked to be about her age, who must be Harrison's wife.

"This is my wife, Marietta," Harrison said, stepping in after her. He smiled down at a little dark-haired toddler in a pretty red dress who was playing with a doll. "And that's our daughter, Melissa. And this is my uncle, Cyrus Damon."

Brie's eyes traveled from smiling Marietta to the little girl, who obviously couldn't care less that she was present, to the older man sitting on a kitchen stool.

She froze when her eyes landed on him.

Cyrus Damon. She'd heard of him before although only in random news items that had never caught her interest. He was a rather eccentric billionaire who ran a huge company that did hotels, restaurants, and tearooms. He'd restored an estate in England and tried to live like eighteenth-century nobility. His family had suffered scandal and tragedy enough to keep them in the papers over the years.

He'd actually told her about a couple of those tragedies, and she still hadn't put the pieces together.

She really should have recognized him.

Cyrus Damon.

Cyrus.

Her Cyrus.

Sitting right there on the stool when she'd thought she'd never see him again.

She literally could not move.

Cyrus was obviously just as taken aback by her presence as she was. He hadn't been expecting her any more than she'd been expecting him. He'd grown very still, staring at her like she was an apparition.

Then he breathed, "Brie."

"Oh," Marietta said with another smile, looking in confusion between Cyrus and Brie. "So you two know each other?"

Seven

Cyrus had been having a very bad day, but was trying to hide it from Harrison, from everyone.

He'd driven up with the others to the bed and breakfast the day before, and he'd been appropriately social and admiring of all the work that had been done. Peter and Kelly Blake had done an excellent job with the renovation, and the contractors and craftsmen they'd employed had obviously all been top-notch. But while he was smiling and making pleasant comments, he was internally waging an endless debate—part of him nearly howling at leaving Brie the way he had and the rest of him explaining over and over again why it was the only choice.

She'd made him happier than he could remember, happier than he'd ever been in his life. But he couldn't make her happy—not for long anyway. And he couldn't start being selfish and thoughtless just because his heart was no longer his.

Only Gordon knew he was secretly suffering. Harrison had asked a couple of times if he was feeling all right, but he'd appeared convinced by Cyrus's responses.

He could do this. He could get through Christmas. Then he could return to England, to his home, and try to remember the man he used to be.

Before these past two weeks. Before Brie.

He was actually almost enjoying watching little Melissa play on the floor in the kitchen, away from the social pressure of the larger crowd. But watching Marietta's obvious joy in her daughter just made him think again about Brie.

Brie should have children. Brie should have a young husband, one who could stand by her side for the rest of her life. He could never be that man for her. He might be able to father children. Men certainly did at his age. But he could never offer her that whole life.

He kept smiling, even at this aching thought.

But his rigid control and his outward façade all cracked like ice when Harrison came back into the kitchen with a young woman who must be Mitchell's sister, whom he vaguely recalled was still expected.

Brie. With Mitchell's dark hair and gray eyes and classic features, with a graceful, Bohemian style that spoke to her artistic nature, and with a warm smile, deep intelligence, and generous spirit that were all her own.

His Brie, whom he had left forever. Standing right in front of him in the kitchen.

He said her name. He knew he did although he wasn't sure how he'd made his voice work.

She didn't say anything. She just went so white he stood up automatically to help her, support her, *something*.

Marietta asked a question with her typical sweetness, smoothing over any rough edges. Then Harrison asked, "Is something wrong?"

Cyrus tried to reply, but there was absolutely nothing to say.

Then Brie made a little sound that was almost like a whimper. She turned on her heel and hurried out of the room.

He started to follow her. Of course he did. She was confused and upset and hurting, and he wanted to take care of her.

But he couldn't. He wasn't allowed. Not anymore. So exerting more strength than he knew he possessed, he very slowly sat back down.

"What's going on?" Harrison demanded, looking baffled and urgent, like there might be a crisis afoot but he couldn't quite find it. "You know each other?"

"Yes," Cyrus managed to say. He had to give his nephew an answer after what they'd just witnessed. "We met in Savannah."

"Oh, well, then what was wrong with her?" Marietta asked. "She looked so shocked and upset."

Harrison had grown still, and Cyrus knew he was putting the pieces together. "Your young woman," he said very softly. "The one Gordon mentioned, who was taking up all your time."

Marietta gave a little gasp and glanced toward the door. "Really?"

Cyrus looked down at Melissa, who was happily rocking her doll like a baby.

"I didn't expect her to be quite so young." Harrison looked like he'd had a blow to the gut.

Cyrus felt a prickle of defensiveness at this comment, but he let it wash over him. Naturally, that would be Harrison's reaction. That would be everyone's reaction. When he'd gone around the city with Brie in the past two weeks, most people hadn't looked at them strangely. The difference in their ages hadn't been shocking or particularly unusual to strangers.

But to family, to those who knew them, it would be a very big deal.

Brie was quite a bit younger even than Harrison. Cyrus should not be romantically attached to her—and age wasn't even the only reason.

"Harry," Marietta chided in a hushed voice. She was the only person in the world who called Harrison that. "Can't you see that they're both really upset? Uncle Cyrus, why don't you go after her? I think she was crying."

Despite all his resolutions, Cyrus almost got up to do just that. He couldn't stand for Brie to be crying. He simply couldn't stand it.

But he managed not to move.

"Uncle Cyrus?" Marietta prompted, looking in concern between him and Harrison beside her. "You don't want to go after her?"

"I... can't."

Marietta grabbed for Harrison's arm, evidently more distressed than ever by the ragged sound of Cyrus's voice. "Harry, do something. Say something."

Harrison cleared his throat. He'd evidently recovered his composure and was watching Cyrus very closely now. "I'm not sure what I can do," he said slowly, thoughtfully. "If he doesn't care about her enough to continue the relationship, then there's no sense in getting her hopes up. She's probably just after his money anyway."

Cyrus stiffened dramatically with a sharp inhale, his eyes flashing at this insult to Brie, which he knew perfectly well wasn't even close to the truth.

Harrison's face changed, and Cyrus realized he'd been testing him, checking to see his responses so he could gauge the nature of Cyrus's feelings.

And Cyrus had fallen right into the trap because his feelings were so far out of control where Brie was concerned.

"So it's like that then," Harrison continued in a different tone. His eyes were unexpectedly gentle. "Then maybe you *should* go after her."

Cyrus let out a breath and let the pain wash over him, knowing he deserved it. "I can't. Please don't ask me again."

He'd always known that he wasn't a perfect man. Sometimes he wasn't even a good one. But despite all the successes and failures and pride and tragedy in his life, he'd always felt whole.

He didn't feel whole anymore.

~

Brie couldn't seem to stop crying.

She'd thought she was in control of her emotions when she arrived at Eden Manor, but obviously she'd just been fooling herself.

Her heart was broken, and it was horrible—and she'd seen it so clearly when she'd encountered Cyrus again in the kitchen.

She knew she should have tried to put on an act so Cyrus wouldn't see how broken she was and so everyone else wouldn't be uncomfortable. But she couldn't. She'd never been a very good actor, and there was just too much emotion to keep down.

She wasn't sure how long had passed when she heard a knock on the door.

She might wish it was Cyrus, but she knew it wasn't. If he'd been coming after her, he would have come right away.

"Go away, Mitchell," she called through the door.

"It's not Mitchell." The voice was female and familiar. "It's Kelly. Are you all right?"

"Oh. Yes."

Kelly evidently took this as an invitation to enter. She opened the door a crack to look in. "Are you okay?"

Brie managed to sit up and wipe at her face. "Yeah. I'm okay. Did Mitchell send you up here?"

"No. He's still in the parlor with Grandmama and the others." Kelly was a slim, attractive girl several years younger than Brie with small glasses and a casual look to her. Her face was concerned as she came to sit on the edge of the bed. "No one sent me up. I was checking on the rooms and heard you crying. What's the matter?"

"I'm not sure how to explain it."

"Just start at the beginning. I have time."

There was no way Brie could start at the beginning—there was too much to say, and it was all still too raw. But she'd always liked Kelly, and she needed to talk to someone. "I, uh, met a man in Savannah I really liked."

"Oh. Yeah. Deanna might have mentioned that." When Kelly realized what she'd said, she hurried on. "That's all she said. She didn't give me any details or anything."

"Yeah, she didn't really know any details. Anyway, we'd agreed we were just having fun for a week or so, and we didn't have any sort of future."

Kelly nodded. "I'm sorry. Did you fall for him anyway?"

"Yeah. Pretty hard. But that's not the worst of it."

"What's the worst of it?"

"I was supposed to never see him again, but he's here."

Kelly gasped. "He's here? Like at Eden Manor?"

"Yes. Here."

Brie could see the wheels turning in Kelly's head. She shook her head as she obviously thought quickly. "But... how... The only unattached man here is... is..."

"Cyrus," Brie said, knowing the reaction she would see on Kelly's face. "It's him."

Kelly was a kindhearted person, but this news was obviously quite a shock. Brie could see quite clearly the succession on emotions on her face. Surprise. Confusion. Disbelief. Then something akin to discomfort.

She couldn't see Brie with Cyrus. Not at all.

Everyone else would have the same reaction as well.

Brie and Cyrus just shouldn't be together—at least no one would ever think they should be.

"Oh," Kelly said at last. "Oh my."

"I know it sounds crazy and no one would expect it, but we really got along... well. We had such a good time together. But I didn't know who he was, and he didn't know who I was, and now... now he still doesn't want me, but it's worse because he's right here."

Kelly's surprise was clearing, and she looked sympathetic again. "I'm really sorry. I didn't mean to make it look like I didn't think you should be—"

"Don't apologize. I know it sounds crazy. I mean, all the differences... But we were really good together. And now we're not together at all."

"I wish I could help."

Brie had slumped down onto the bed again, but now she sat up quickly. "You can't tell Mitchell. Please don't tell him. He would... Please don't tell him."

"I won't. But maybe you should talk to Mr. Dam—to Cyrus. He's seemed really down since he got here yesterday. Nothing obvious, but it's like he's always brooding about something he's trying to hide. Maybe he didn't want things to end either."

"I wish it were that easy." Despite herself, the thought that Cyrus had been depressed made her feel a little better. It wasn't like she wanted him to suffer, but at least leaving her hadn't been easy for him. At least she wasn't as foolish as to have fallen into a one-sided thing.

There was another knock on the door, and Marietta stuck her head in. "Brie? I'm just checking on you. Just tell me if you want me to leave."

"No, you can come in. Thank you."

Marietta's eyes were deeply sympathetic as she sat in the upright chair. "Are you okay?"

Brie nodded, sitting up again. "I'll be okay." She let out a breath. "So he didn't want to talk to me?"

Marietta shook her head. "He wants to, but he won't."

"He said from the beginning that we had no future. I only have myself to blame for... letting myself hope for more." Brie's eyes strayed to the closed bedroom door. "Is he okay?"

Marietta gave a little shrug. "I really don't know. I've known him for a long time, but I've never seen him like this. He's always been a good man, but for a long time there was this hardness inside him, underneath all the manners and sophistication. But he's been changing over the past few years. He's closer now to his family than he ever was before. And now... now it seems like he's changed even more, even since I last saw him a few weeks ago."

Brie was almost hanging on the words. She wanted to know this about Cyrus. She wanted to know everything. "But I don't think he's going to change his mind about this."

"I don't know. It doesn't seem like it, and he's always been impossibly stubborn about what he believes is right. But I wonder... it's almost like he thinks he doesn't..."

Brie leaned forward. "He thinks he doesn't what?"

Marietta shook her head helplessly. "I guess I don't know. I'm sorry, Brie. I wish I could help."

"You have helped," Brie said, reaching out to put her hand on the other woman's arm and then reaching over to squeeze Kelly's arm too. "Thank you both."

"So what are you going to do?" Kelly asked.

Brie shrugged and wiped at her face. "What can I do? I'm going to be a grown-up and get on with my life. I just have to get through Christmas first."

Kelly stood up. "Well, here. Come and pat Igor's head."

"Igor?"

"He's a stuffed cat. He was a gift from my grandmother, and we had to explain his presence in the house, so we put him on a pedestal in the hall and we tell everyone that patting his head brings luck."

Brie and Marietta followed Kelly out into the back hallway, where Igor had been given a position of honor in a glass case on an ornate pedestal.

Brie had been picturing a stuffed animal cat, but that wasn't what Igor was. He was a dead Siamese cat who had been stuffed into a living pose and was staring out at the world with creepy glass eyes.

"Oh my!" Marietta breathed.

"Pat his head," Kelly instructed, opening the top of the case.

Marietta reached inside and gave the furry head a little pat, and then Brie did as well.

"Does it really bring luck?" Brie asked.

Kelly gave an adorable little shrug. "It hasn't yet. But there has to be a first time, right?"

Several hours later, Brie was staring up at a mural on the ceiling of the dining room.

It was close to a traditional Victorian sky scene but was filled with light and life and unexpected details, and it was absolutely gorgeous.

As strange as it sounded, Brie was almost positive that the artist who had done this ceiling was the same one who had painted her lovely little fishing pond.

The room was crowded, as were the parlor and hall and kitchen. The Blakes had invited quite a few people to their Christmas Eve party, in addition to the guests who were already present. Brie had made it through the afternoon by avoiding Cyrus and pasting on a smile anytime she felt too emotional. But she would be really glad when this party was over and she could be alone in her room.

She was still staring up at the ceiling when a woman came up beside her. "Do you like it?"

Brie straightened her head and smiled at the woman, who looked around her own age, with lovely, long hair and a delicate look about her. "Yes. It's amazing. Do you know who did it?"

"Her name is Cassandra Vance."

Brie gasped. "I knew it! I *knew* it!"

The woman drew her brows together. "What did you know?"

"I have a painting by her—of a fishing pond. It's so amazing, and I knew she must have painted this ceiling too." She gave the other woman a smile. "Sorry. I'm Brie."

The woman shook her hand. "I'm Cassandra."

141

It took a moment for the name to sink it. "Cass—you're not…."

"I am," Cassandra admitted. "And I'm absolutely thrilled that you love the ceiling and that you bought that painting in Savannah. It's one of my favorites."

"I didn't exactly buy it," Brie explained, prompted by her innate honesty. "It was a gift. But it was… It's so special to me. Thank you for painting it."

"You're welcome. Thank you for loving it. That fishing pond is special to me too."

Brie was still putting pieces together. "Vance? You're not related to Silas Vance, are you? The one who did the stained glass?"

"He's my husband." Cassandra's face took on that pleased pride that Brie always saw on Mitchell's face when he talked about Deanna's beadwork. "He's here tonight, but he's probably hiding out somewhere. He doesn't like crowds."

"I'd love to talk to him sometime. I do stained glass too."

"He'll definitely want to talk to you then."

Cassandra looked around, evidently in search of her husband. And Brie looked around as well.

She knew Cyrus wasn't in sight. She'd known exactly where he was every moment of the afternoon and evening. She looked around anyway, her eyes landing on two couples who were standing near the fireplace. She'd met them briefly. One couple were the contractors who had done the work on the house, and the other couple had done the landscaping. Or something like that. She couldn't remember their names, but they'd seemed very nice.

She focused on them now, standing together, laughing at a private joke, evidently very good friends with each other.

The women were both pretty, and the dark-haired woman was pregnant. The men were strong and young and attractive and healthy—clearly in love with their wives.

And it struck Brie then that one or the other of those men were the kind of husband she'd always assumed she'd eventually have. In any vision of her future, she'd pictured being part of a couple like that.

She'd thought that life would be hers.

And she realized in that moment that she didn't need that life. She didn't want that life. She didn't want that kind of husband.

She wanted a life with Cyrus.

And she didn't care if he was so much older than her or rich and notorious or with a reputation for eccentricity. She didn't care if he was weighed down by guilt and tragedy, so much that it was still dogging his steps, his decisions. She didn't care if the rest of the world would automatically assume she was just after his money, and they would judge her for it.

She didn't *care*.

She wanted the man she'd known for the past two weeks, no matter what else came with him.

Because she hadn't made a mistake. In everything he did—even in saying good-bye—it was so clear to her that Cyrus cared more about her than he did about himself.

She was almost breathless from the revelation and nearly forgot that Cassandra was still beside her.

"It's strange sometimes, isn't it?" Cassandra said softly.

Brie turned and saw that the other woman was staring at the same young couples she herself had been a minute ago. "What is?"

"When you're looking at a life you might have had, knowing you'll never have it—but also knowing the one you have is the right one. For *you*."

Brie wasn't sure if Cassandra had read her mind or if she was thinking of something different. She seemed to be staring at the belly of the pregnant woman, so Brie decided there was a story there she just didn't know.

She didn't have time right now to know it though.

She had something else she had to do.

She excused herself and walked across the hall to the parlor, where she knew Cyrus was. He was there, sitting in a chair with a glass of wine in his hand. By himself. Watching the world go on around him.

His eyes strayed over to where she was standing but then immediately looked away.

She took a deep breath and walked toward him.

He turned his eyes back to her as she got closer, and she could see the question in his face. Without speaking, she reached down and took his free hand and then pulled him out of the chair, out of the room, out the doors that led onto the side porch.

"Brie, what are you doing?" he asked, putting his glass of wine on the railing of the porch. "It's cold out here, and you don't have a coat on."

"I'm fine. And I want to talk to you."

His face softened slightly as he gazed down at her. "Dear heart, we've already said everything there is to say."

"No, we haven't. You've said what *you* want to say, but I haven't. And I have some things to say now."

The sound of laughter from right inside the door startled her by its closeness. This was between her and Cyrus. She didn't want anyone else to hear. She took his hand again and pulled him down the steps and across the yard toward the lake. It felt like winter here, when it hadn't in Savannah.

"Brie, it's too cold out here."

"Would you stop saying that? I'm not cold at all." She was speaking the truth. She didn't feel chilled. She felt on fire with everything she was feeling.

They stopped close to a bench swing, and Brie turned to face him. Then it all came pouring out. "I don't care how old you are. I just don't care. I don't care if you're twenty or thirty or fifty years older than me. That just doesn't matter to me. Age is meaningless to the way we are together. You know it's true. You felt it just like I did for these past two weeks. I'm not a girl anymore. I'm almost thirty years old. I'm an adult, and you get to a point where the age difference just doesn't matter anymore."

Cyrus closed his eyes briefly and said very softly, "It may not matter now, but it will eventually. Twenty years from now when I'm in my seventies and you're... not. It's going to matter then."

She brushed his words away. "You don't get to decide that for me. What we have is special. You know it is."

"Of course I know it is." He started to reach for her face but then drew his hand away.

"Then why can't we have more than those two weeks?"

"You know why. You know who I am now. Even without the age difference, we're worlds apart."

"None of that matters." She was almost crying again with her urgency. She reached out to take his shirt in her hands, clutching it helplessly. "Can't you see? I just don't care about Cyrus Damon. He's not important enough to get in the way of us. I want to be with you. Just you. Cyrus. *My* Cyrus."

Cyrus's face twisted slightly, and he made a strange little moan in his throat. He reached out for her again, and this time Brie knew he was going to kiss her. She could see it in his eyes.

He felt the same way she did. She *knew* it.

But he turned away from her with a sudden jerk of his body.

Her tears started to fall again, even before she heard him say, "I'm so sorry, dear heart. I wouldn't have hurt you for anything. But I'm absolutely convinced that you'll hurt even more if I give in on this. My life will not be good for you. I know you say you don't care about all the rest of it right now, but one day you will. You'll suffer because you're attached to me, and I refuse to let that happen."

"But I want to suffer *with* you. I want to do everything with you. Please, please let me, Cyrus."

She was still holding on to one little flicker of hope that simply wouldn't die, but it went dark when Cyrus shook his head, an iron will she'd never seen before in his eyes. "I can't. You've been my most precious gift, but I can't."

She was crying helplessly now, no way to hold it back. Cyrus gently brushed her hair back from her face. He kissed both of her cheeks, her temple, her lips.

Then he turned and walked away, leaving her alone in the dark.

∼

Forty-five minutes later, Cyrus was staring in confusion at his empty suitcase.

It shouldn't be empty because he'd just packed it.

He blinked a couple of times and then turned his head when Gordon entered the room. He'd been at Eden Manor ever since Cyrus had arrived, but he'd kept out of sight, no matter how many times Cyrus told him he was welcome to join the others.

"What happened to my clothes?" Cyrus demanded.

"I put them where they belonged, in the closet and the dresser."

"I mean just now. I had them packed, and now they're…"

"Back where they belong," Gordon said blandly.

Cyrus almost groaned. He couldn't remember anything hurting the way watching Brie cry earlier had, and he had no emotional energy left to handle even a silly argument. "Pack them up again," he said curtly. "I'm leaving."

"It's Christmas Eve."

"I know that. But I can't stay here. It will make things even harder for Brie. I'll spend Christmas with Lucy and Benjamin. I need to leave."

"You know what I think about that."

"Yes, I do. But this is my decision. It's made, and it's final, and everyone needs to stop trying to talk me out of it."

Gordon didn't react to the harshness of his tone. "Is it possible," he began mildly, "that if everyone who cares about you disagrees with your decision, that your decision should perhaps be rethought."

"I have rethought it. I've rethought it over and over again, and I always end up in the same place. I can't be with her. I have to leave."

Gordon didn't say anything. He also didn't make a move to start packing up the clothes again, so Cyrus went to the closet to do so himself.

When the silence was simply too oppressive, he burst out, "I can't, Gordon! What kind of hypocrite would I be if, after years of holding everyone around me to impossibly high standards, so much so that I've hurt the people I love, I just throw all my standards out the window because there's something I want so much. What kind of hypocrite would I be?"

There was a long pause before Gordon answered. "Not a hypocrite at all. Simply a man who has changed."

The words startled Cyrus. He paused in grabbing a couple of shirts off hangers in the closet, staring blindly in Gordon's direction.

He wasn't sure what he would have said then if there hadn't been a knock on the door.

Harrison came in without waiting for an invitation.

Cyrus sat down in a slump on an upright chair. "Not you too, Harrison. How many times do I have to explain to you that my mind is made up?"

"Not to me," Harrison said with a shake of his head. It was only then that Cyrus saw he had a phone in his hand. "It was an emergency. I had to bring in the big guns. He's always been better with people than me."

Cyrus frowned as Harrison handed him the phone. He put it to his ear automatically. "Hello?"

"Lord Uncle?" came a familiar voice.

Cyrus let out a breath. "Andrew." Another one of his nephews. Harrison's brother.

"Yeah, it's me. Harrison said there was an emergency, and Laurel and I might need to fly in from Santorini."

"You do not need to fly in. There is no emergency."

Andrew was silent for a moment before he asked, "So you fell for someone after all this time?"

Cyrus's throat tightened, and he couldn't manage an answer.

"I guess that's a yes. Listen, I don't know the whole situation, but I don't care who she is. You deserve to be happy, and you've never let yourself be happy before. And if anyone gives you grief about it, you can move to Santorini and live with me, Laurel, and the dogs. Theo sleeps on a bed now—I mean a real person bed—but I'm sure he would share with you and your girl."

Cyrus gave a hoarse huff of amusement. No one in the world but Andrew could make him laugh, even when his heart was breaking. "Thank you, Andrew."

"No problem. You know, I always knew you were secretly a rogue."

The word was an almost nostalgic callback to some of the things Cyrus had called Andrew years ago. His throat hurt from too many emotions at once as Cyrus said, "I learned from the best."

He'd relaxed slightly when he said good-bye and handed Harrison the phone. Gordon had left the room sometime during the phone call.

Letting out a long breath, Cyrus turned to Harrison, who'd lowered himself to sit on the bed across from him. "Harrison. I do appreciate the effort."

"But?"

"You shouldn't be helping me with this after the way I treated you and Marietta. I'm not lost to the irony, you know."

"Please. That's ancient history. It's forgiven. It's not important anymore." When Cyrus started to argue, Harrison reached out a hand and touched Cyrus's wrist. "You know very well that's not how love works."

Cyrus couldn't speak for a moment.

Harrison went on. "I was surprised at first, but that wasn't my final response. I don't give a damn about who you fall for or who you choose to love, just as long as she wants the best for you. I'm happy if you're happy. That's how it works."

Cyrus was so emotional he could barely breathe. He stared down at his hands with blurry eyes.

"Are you happy?" Harrison asked after a long moment.

"No."

"I want you to be. Andrew wants you to be. Gordon wants you to be. Ben and Jonathan and all our wives and kids. Aunt Lucy. All of us want you to be happy. And it seems pretty clear that's what Brie wants too. You're the only one who doesn't want that."

Cyrus lifted his eyes at this, vaguely surprised to see that Harrison's expression was very kind.

"You think because you've made mistakes in the past that you don't deserve to be happy. The least you can do is admit it."

It was the same thing Gordon had tried to tell him more than once. Harrison was right. Gordon was right. He'd been sacrificing everything to get the future he thought he deserved.

But any other option was absolutely terrifying.

He said, "So I just shouldn't care about what will happen to Brie if she's with me? How the world will believe she's a shallow fortune-hunter? A trophy wife?"

"If she doesn't care about that, then I don't see why you should."

"How will she feel twenty years from now, when—"

"Listen to yourself," Harrison interrupted. "Twenty years from now. You're willing to give up twenty years with

150

her on the off-chance she might have some extra difficulty as you get older? *Twenty years with her.*"

Twenty years. With Brie. Or more. Maybe even twice that amount of time.

Cyrus wanted it so much he couldn't breathe, he couldn't see straight.

And it seemed like the universe—like everyone he cared about—was conspiring to make it happen.

To give him the happiness he wouldn't give himself.

Cyrus stood up, wanting to find Brie, wanting to take her in his arms, to never let her go.

But he just couldn't seem to make his body work. His will had always been so much stronger than his heart.

Harrison stood up too. "Listen to me." He put a hand on his shoulder until Cyrus was looking him in the eyes. "It's never been about deserving. I know this better than anyone. My name is Harrison Damon, and that wouldn't mean anything without you."

It felt for a moment like Cyrus cracked inside. He took a ragged breath and turned his head toward the door.

"She's down by the lake," Harrison said in a different tone although still hoarse from the moment before. He'd evidently read a resolution on Cyrus's face. "You should go find her."

Cyrus lowered his brows. "What? Why is she still outside? It's too cold to be out there so long, and she doesn't have a coat!"

Harrison laughed and reached into the closet to grab one of Cyrus's. "Then maybe you should bring her one."

Eight

Brie was huddled up on the bench swing next to the lake, staring out at the starlight and moonlight reflected on the still water.

She wasn't crying anymore, but she was shivering in her thin sweater. She just couldn't bring herself to move, much less go back inside and rejoin the others.

It felt like if she just stayed here, then maybe she could hold back time and she wouldn't have to go through Christmas day, the rest of this year, the whole next year, the rest of her life without Cyrus.

A little voice at the back of her head was laughing at her, telling her this was a very dramatic reaction to a man she'd only known for two weeks.

She didn't care about that voice. It didn't know anything.

It was wrong, so wrong—an injustice so clear she could feel it shuddering inside her—that Cyrus hadn't changed his mind and let himself be with her.

She hoped he was okay.

He would probably leave, not wanting to make Christmas awkward for her. He would go back to that archaic mansion of his in England and try to forget the man he'd been with her this month, the man he'd finally let himself be.

It was just wrong, but wrong things happened in the world all the time. Cyrus might have been right in his theological reflections. Maybe power would always trump grace in the workings of the universe.

She was mulling over this—her mind drifting into odd, disconnected ramblings—when she heard a slight sound from behind her. She didn't turn around. It was probably the wind ruffling the tree branches. Or maybe a raccoon, snuffling out something to eat in the dark.

Then she heard a voice. "Brie! Brie, what are you doing out here in the cold?"

She was so startled and disoriented she just stared as Cyrus hurried up to the swing, wrapping a coat around her shoulders and sitting down beside her.

The coat was warm, and it smelled like him. She pulled it tighter around her shoulders.

Then she burst into tears.

"Oh no. Please don't." He pulled her into his arms, rather awkwardly since they were both still sitting on the rocking bench swing, and she sobbed into his chest.

"I'm sorry. I can't help it," she gasped, completely out of control but still trying to explain her breakdown to him. "You keep breaking my heart."

"I know. I know. I'm not going to do it again."

She almost choked when the soft words made their way into her clouded mind. She pulled away and stared at his face reflected in the moonlight. His eyes were beautiful chocolate brown. Soft and very tender. Stripped bare from the internal defenses he'd always worn like armor.

"Do you still believe in second chances, Brie?" he asked, his mouth turning up in the slightest of smiles.

"Yes, I do," she rasped. "I always have."

"Then I would like to ask for a second chance with you if you would extend me that grace."

The careful, almost formal words were a jarring contrast to the naked emotion in his eyes, and it completely undid Brie again. Her whole body shook with barely suppressed sobs, and she threw herself back into his arms.

"Oh, my dear heart," Cyrus murmured, tightening his arms around her almost painfully. "If this is your answer, I'm not sure what it means."

"It means yes!" she burst out, finally able to straighten up again. She was smiling like a fool now through her tears. "I told you I believe in grace. I told you it was the most important thing, the thing that makes the world beautiful. You're the one who didn't believe in it."

Cyrus lifted his hands to cup her face, like she was precious, like she was the most precious thing in the world. And he murmured thickly, "I believe in it now."

So she was smiling and crying and shaking and overflowing with joy as he pulled her into a soft kiss. She wrapped her arms around him as she kissed him back, causing his coat to slide off her shoulders.

Even as he was kissing her, Cyrus kept pulling the coat back up to keep her warm.

After a few emotional and rather messy minutes, they finally pulled apart. With a silent, mutual understanding, they rearranged themselves so they were leaning back against the swing. Cyrus's arm was wrapped around her, and she was pressed up at his side. Brie even managed to put her arms through the sleeves of the coat so it wouldn't keep sliding off. It was too big, but it was warm and heavy—and *his*. She was very happy.

"I'm a little afraid to go inside," she admitted after a minute. "I feel like everyone in there knows what's happening out here."

Cyrus chuckled softly. "I'm afraid they probably do. Your brother isn't likely to be happy that you've attached yourself to an old man."

"Don't call yourself that." She stroked his chest. "You're not *that* old."

He gave her a very warm smile, a particular smolder in his eyes that quickened her pulse.

"Mitchell will get over it," she continued, snuggling up beside him again. "And I wouldn't want you to be even a year younger. Every year you've lived has made you *you*."

She could feel him smiling although she was gazing out at the lake again.

They sat in silence for a long time, wrapped up in each other. Brie stared at how the moonlight and starlight glazed the water with pure, white light. Occasionally, in the grass or on the bare tree branches hanging over them, she could see a glint and sparkle of frost.

Finally she murmured, "It's a silver kind of night."

He brushed a kiss into her hair. "Yes. It is. It's beautiful."

"And who's to say that's less precious than gold?"

Early the next morning, Cyrus woke up without circulation in his arm.

He felt warm and cramped and relaxed and quite pleased with his position, despite his prickling arm. Brie was snuggled up beside him, still sound asleep.

Very carefully he eased his arm out from under her and tried to shake it gently to restore the blood flow. He didn't want to wake her. They hadn't gone to sleep until late. When they'd finally come inside, the party was breaking up, and people were drifting off to their rooms. Cyrus had spoken briefly to Harrison and gone to his room alone. He didn't want to part ways with Brie, but there were too many people mingling in the hallways to do anything else—including members of his family and hers.

He'd always been intensely private, and it was no one else's business how he behaved with the woman he loved.

An hour or so later, after the house had become quiet, there had been a light tap on the door. He hadn't been asleep and, when he opened the door, Brie had slipped into his room.

They'd made love in slow, silent tenderness before they'd gone to sleep together.

Despite his attempts not to wake her, Brie started to stir now beside him. She made a few little mouth noises and then opened her eyes.

She smiled at him groggily when she saw he was watching her.

"I'm sorry to wake you," he said.

"Don't be." She burrowed beside him as he wrapped his still prickly arm around her. "I'm glad to wake up today."

"Merry Christmas."

"You too." She was smiling, beaming, glowing—even though her eyes were still sleepy.

He kissed the crown of her head, his chest brimming with deep emotion he'd never believed he was capable of before. "You look happy."

"I am. So, so happy." She tilted her head to check his expression. "Aren't you?"

"You have no idea how much. Although my arm went to sleep from you lying on it all night."

She giggled and, to his surprise, crawled over his body, snuggling up against his other side. "Then we'll have to change positions to give that arm a rest."

He laughed softly and pulled her into a hug with both arms, both the prickly and the nonprickly one.

After a minute, when both of them had relaxed under the covers, he said, "Maybe we should talk about a few things."

"About what?"

"About what we're going to do after today. We have a few things to sort through if we're going to make this relationship work."

"Like what?"

"Like the fact that I live in England most of the time and you live in Savannah."

"Oh. Right. I guess that is kind of an issue."

He pulled back enough to look at her face. "I'm sure we can work it out. A lot of my business is centered in England, but much of the time I can work remotely. I don't mind spending a lot of time in Savannah, as much time as I possibly can."

"That's really generous of you. And I could go over to England when I'm between jobs. Although..." She trailed off as if she were suddenly afraid to finish the sentence.

"Although what?" he prompted.

"Although I don't have a job right now, which means I'm pretty flexible in terms of location. I supposed there might be churches in England, around you, that need restoration work." She gave him a quick, self-conscious look. "If that's not rushing you or anything."

He gasped audibly, his whole body freezing as he realized what she was saying.

Seeing his reaction and evidently misreading it, she hurried on, "It was just an idea. I know we've only been together for a couple of weeks, and my moving there is probably too huge a step. I was just thinking, since I don't have

157

a job here, maybe I could find one there. But I didn't mean to pressure you or make things too serious too quickly. It's probably better for me to just stay in Savannah until—"

"Brie," he interrupted, forgetting his manners in his earnestness. "I would love for you to move close to me. I just didn't dare to hope for it."

She let out a gusty sigh, her face starting to glow again. "Oh, thank goodness. I thought I'd pushed things too far. I know I should be more careful, but I've never been good at that. I just get so excited."

He chuckled and reached over to stroke her cheek. "Dear heart, you don't have to be careful with me. I've never been a casual person—about anything—and my feelings for you are as serious as feelings can be."

Her breath hitched, and her cheeks reddened a little more. "Oh. Good."

"You do know I'm falling in love with you, don't you?" he murmured.

She made a soft noise in her throat, her eyes suddenly glistening with unshed tears. "I'm glad I'm not alone in it."

He kissed her slowly, deeply, but they didn't take it any further. When they pulled apart, Brie was smiling again. "So, back to the original topic, if I can find a job over there, I'd be very happy to move. I love Savannah, but it's not like I have to live there the rest of my life. I'd just want any job I have to be a real one and not something engineered by you to get me over there."

Cyrus couldn't help but laugh since he'd been starting to search his mind for favors he could call in to get Brie exactly the kind of position she would most want. "All right. We'll start looking for you a real job as soon as the holidays are over."

They lay together for a few more minutes until Cyrus heard a few sounds from elsewhere in the house. He glanced at the clock. Breakfast wasn't until eight, so they still had over an hour.

"I guess I should go back to my own room," Brie said, following his gaze, "before people start to get up. I'm not too keen on everyone knowing I spent the night in here."

Cyrus couldn't help but be relieved by this sentiment. "We'll have plenty of privacy soon enough."

She beamed at him, giving a quick kiss before she got out of bed. She was still wearing her nightgown although it was rather wrinkled from their activities in bed last night. Her body was slim and graceful and beautiful, and Cyrus couldn't help but enjoy it as she smoothed down her messy hair and the fabric of her gown. Her tousled appearance, the glow to her skin, and the languid satisfaction in her mood all testified to the fact that she'd had a very good night, and he couldn't smother the ripple of pleased pride at the knowledge that he was the one who had given it to her.

She pulled on the robe and slippers she'd worn to come into his room and went to the door.

She blew him a silent kiss before she peeked out, checking the hallway to make sure it was empty.

Then she slipped out of the room.

~

Brie was leaving her room less than an hour later, having showered and dressed, when she saw Cyrus closing his bedroom door behind him. He was dressed too, and he looked his normal, expensive, sophisticated, and well-tailored self.

He gave her a very intimate smile when he saw her that made her blush. "Merry Christmas," he said in his normal tone, as if they'd just seen each other for the first time that morning.

There were a couple of people walking down the stairs in front of them. It looked like Deanna and her grandmother, old Mrs. Beaufort.

"Merry Christmas to you too," she said, ducking her head and hiding a smile.

She started down the stairs, Cyrus behind her, but she came to a stop when she realized Mrs. Beaufort was waiting on the landing. Brie hadn't seen the older woman the evening before because she'd gone to bed very early, just after the party had started.

"Good morning, young lady," the tiny old woman said in an imperious tone, giving her a nod but not a smile.

"Good morning," she replied.

Then Brie realized the woman wasn't actually waiting for her. She was waiting for Cyrus. Because as soon as Cyrus had reached the landing, Grandmama squared her shoulders and tilted her head to glare up at him. "Young man, you are a disgrace."

Cyrus gave a little twitch of surprise, his eyes widening.

"Grandmama!" Deanna whispered, her expression vaguely appalled.

Mrs. Beaufort ignored her granddaughter and kept glaring at Cyrus. "Cavorting about with a woman half your age. You should be ashamed of yourself, sir."

Cyrus had recovered from his surprise, and now he gave the old woman a cool look. He spoke in his most formal, arrogant tone as he replied, "And you, madam, should exert a herculean effort and mind your own business."

Grandmama Beaufort was speechless. It was the first time Brie had ever seen her so.

Deanna's eyes were as round as saucers, and she had to raise a hand to hide the smile that was spreading slowly across her face. She and Brie exchanged looks of amazed hilarity.

Then Cyrus glanced back at Brie as if nothing at all had happened. "Shall we go down to breakfast, love?"

Brie hurried to take the hand Cyrus had extended, and they walked down the stairs together.

As they descended, Brie heard Mrs. Beaufort say to Deanna on the landing. "Well, I never! I thought he still needed a good push in the right direction, but I see now they've already sorted themselves out."

~

Cyrus Damon felt like a new man that day.

He had breakfast with the others, and then they all went into the parlor to open presents in front of a roaring fire, which admittedly got a bit warm since the day wasn't nearly as cold as the night before. The children—little Melissa and Rose and James's children—screamed with laughter and pleasure at all their new treasures, and eventually the larger group broke up into smaller groups to amuse themselves until dinnertime.

Cyrus took some time to call the rest of his family— Lucy, Benjamin and Mandy, Andrew and Laurel, his other nephew Jonathan and his wife, Sarah, and their two sons. They were all happy to hear from him, and he knew their affection was genuine.

And Brie was beside him the whole time, leaning against him or holding his hand or meeting his eyes with special, little looks that only the two of them recognized.

They found Gordon, who was keeping out of sight, despite their continued requests that he join them. They exchanged presents with him, and before he left them, Gordon clapped a light hand on Cyrus's shoulder.

It meant something. It meant a lot.

In the early afternoon, he and Brie went outside to sit on the swing next to the lake so they could have some time alone. They talked about how they would spend the rest of the holiday season. They talked about the kinds of jobs she could be looking for in England. They talked about the brand new year coming, a second chance, a gift he never would have expected.

The sun was bright, and the sky was clear, so the afternoon was a golden one, despite the light chill in the air.

Cyrus was washed with wave after wave of feeling, of joy—so much so it would have normally terrified him as he waited for the universe to balance the scales. But today he didn't try to fight it. He welcomed it, knew it for one of the blessings of a universe whose edges didn't always have to be sharp.

There could be golden days like this one in the world. Places with soft, forested hills, sparkling lakes, houses full of warmth and history and generations of human lives. Spaces of quiet, of peace. Family ties that gave shape to one's world. Loyalty and devotion when one didn't deserve it. Love that gilded the world like the sunshine.

The universe could be golden, hope glowing with the light of the sun.

It was golden today. Right now. It wasn't perfection, but it spoke of something like grace.

It made him believe in it.

Some of the days after this one might be hard. Naturally, those days would come. But Cyrus now had hope that the bad could be outweighed, transformed, *covered* by the good.

Epilogue

One year later

As Brie woke up, even before she managed to get her eyes opened, she had the strongest impression that something really good was happening today.

She enjoyed the sensation for a minute, feeling cozy and relaxed and like there was no pressing reason to move quite yet. She was in the big bed in the huge master suite in Damon Manor, Cyrus's vast, gorgeous estate about an hour outside of London. The sheets on this bed were the best sheets she'd ever slept on. She'd never known sheets could feel so nice against her skin. Even after sleeping on them for so many months, they still felt luxurious to her.

She finally woke up enough to roll over and open her eyes, smiling as she saw Cyrus sprawled out beside her, wearing the pajamas she'd given him last night.

He was still sound asleep, and he tended to run hot, so he'd pushed the covers down to his waist sometime during the night. The pajamas were red flannel and were covered by the repeated image of a puppy in a Santa hat, his tongue lolling out and his eyes way too big for his head.

She'd thought they were cute and funny, so she'd given them to Cyrus as a Christmas Eve / anniversary gift.

She couldn't believe he'd actually put them on and then kept them on all night.

They'd been together exactly a year now. That was one of the reasons she was so happy.

The other reason was that it was Christmas, and she was excited about the day.

They weren't going to have a big celebration this year. Only Harrison, Marietta, and Melissa were here. Cyrus had tried to get his other nephews to visit, but they'd all had other plans. Brie wished that Mitchell and Deanna had been able to come over for the holiday, but there had been some sort of issue involving Grandmama that had kept them in Savannah.

But still… Brie was sure they'd have a good day today, even with a small group.

As she lay on her side, watching Cyrus sleep, she felt a clench of feeling in her chest. He usually woke up before she did, so she didn't get to see him sleeping like this very often. He needed to shave, and his hair was ruffled, and he looked adorably incongruous in those ridiculous pajamas. One of his hands was clenched in the duvet.

She loved him so much.

It had been April before she'd been able to find a good job here in England, so the first few months of this year had been long and frustrating, as they'd been living on different continents. Cyrus would have been happy to support her until she found a job, but she'd felt a little strange about that. She'd wanted to pay her own way—at least while they were dating. He would never have treated her anything like a mistress, but the idea of it had still made her uncomfortable. So they'd lived with an ocean between them, flying back and forth as often as they could.

Then one of Cyrus's contacts had told them about restoration work beginning on a small cathedral in a village about forty minutes away. The work was supposed to last for at least two years, and there were more stained glass windows in the building than Brie could have dreamed of. She didn't actually like her boss very much, but that was a minor aggravation.

She was still renting a tiny cottage in a village nearby although now she spent most nights over here.

Cyrus would always be old-fashioned. She knew he'd be uncomfortable about her actually moving in with him while they weren't married, so she never suggested giving up her own place.

She'd been keeping still on purpose so she wouldn't wake him up, but he started to stir anyway. She watched as he blinked and stretched slightly and then turned his head to look in her direction.

He smiled—that very tender smile that almost no one ever saw but her.

"Merry Christmas," she murmured, after swallowing over the silliest lump of emotion in her throat.

"Merry Christmas," he said in return, sounding typically composed and articulate, even after being awake for less than a minute. "Although I think I'm more prepared for it than you are since I'm wearing my Christmas pajamas."

She giggled helplessly and was about to scoot over to kiss him when she rethought the wisdom of such a course of action. Instead, she said, "I'll be right back," and rolled out of bed and hurried into the bathroom.

She used the bathroom, washed her face, and brushed her teeth. Then she checked herself out in the mirror. She had on one of the soft cotton nightgowns she usually wore, this one blue with pretty ruffles on the straps. It was wrinkled though, and her hair was a mess.

She tried smoothing both of them down, but it didn't help. She still looked rumpled and not particularly sexy.

Nothing to do about it though. Cyrus wouldn't like dramatic, sexy lingerie even if she'd ever wanted to wear it. It wasn't her, and it wasn't him.

This morning, he'd have to make do with her looking like this.

They hadn't had sex in two weeks.

He'd had a really busy month with work, and he'd been unusually stressed for the past few weeks. It was all she could do to get him to relax at night so he could sleep. He had no extra energy or focus for sex.

She wasn't particularly worried. Most couples went through ups and downs in terms of sex, and overall she was quite satisfied in that department. Cyrus might not be ready to go at the drop of a hat like a younger man would be, but he was attentive and thoughtful and generous and incredibly romantic.

Still, after two weeks, she wouldn't complain about having sex this morning.

She left the bathroom and returned to bed, pleased to see a warm look in Cyrus's eyes as she approached. She got into bed on her side and started to crawl over toward him.

Before she could reach him, though, he said, "Well, now I have to brush my teeth too. I'm not going to be the only one with bad breath."

Brie flopped over in another fit of giggles while Cyrus got up and went to the bathroom to take care of business. He returned after only a minute and was smiling as he climbed back into bed beside her.

She rolled over, moving over him to grab the lapels of his top. "Now," she said. "I thought I might take your new pajamas off."

"I believe that would be an excellent plan," he murmured, his brown eyes hot and soft both as he gazed up at her.

She had a very good time taking off his pajamas, and then he pulled her gown up over her head. She was poised above him, and for just a moment her breath hitched when she saw the look in his eyes as he gazed at her flushed face and naked body.

Adoration. That was the only way to describe it.

She leaned over to kiss him, and they kissed for a long time, stroking each other until both of them were urgent and aroused. Then she lined herself up so she could ride him, and he kept watching her with that same adoring look as she moved above him.

After a few minutes, when the motion wasn't enough for her, he found her clit and rubbed it skillfully until the pleasure broke inside her. Then he turned her over onto her back, and she wrapped her legs around him as he built up a steady, pleasing rhythm. They kissed on and off, and she was filled by him, surrounded by him, so incredibly loved by him.

He brought her to orgasm again before he took his own release. He was never loud in bed, but his voice was hoarse, raw, filled with naked need as he gasped, "Brie, dear heart," just before he came inside her.

They'd stopped using a condom several months ago, so she felt the wetness of his release as they gasped and softened in each other's arms afterward.

"I love you, dear heart," he murmured when he'd finally found his voice. He'd rolled over onto his back, taking her with him, and now he was gently stroking her hair, her back, her bottom.

She smiled against his chest. "I love you too. So, so much."

"I'm sorry it's been so long since we've done that."

"Don't apologize. I know you've been busy and stressed. It hasn't been *that* long."

"It's been too long. I don't want you to miss out on anything, not if it's in my power to give you."

She raised her head to look down at his face, her hair falling over her shoulders, brushing against his chest. "Are you serious? I'm not missing out on anything—not anything—I want. Honestly, other women can only dream of having it as good as I do."

He chuckled appreciatively and stroked her cheek gently. "I don't want other men to even dream about you."

She turned her head so she could kiss his hand. But her voice was light as she said, "I don't think anyone ever really dreamed about me."

"I did. I dreamed about you for years, long before I ever found you."

Brie made a silly sound in her throat as she processed the words. Then she had no choice but to kiss him again, long and deep and slow.

They were still tangled together, both of them in a rather sappy haze, when there was a tap on the bedroom door.

Brie squeaked and pulled the covers up over her naked body.

Cyrus chuckled. "It's just Gordon. I asked him to bring breakfast up to the room this morning." He reached down to grab his pajamas pants from the floor and pulled them on.

Brie wasn't comfortable being naked in the room with anyone else, even under the covers, so she quickly pulled her gown back on over her head as Cyrus got up to open the door.

He could have just called out to let Gordon in. She wasn't sure why he'd gotten up. But she figured it didn't matter when Gordon came in rolling a lovely cart of coffee, juice, fruit, pastries, and bacon.

"Oh, yum," she said, getting excited about the food. She sat up on the edge of the bed. "Thank you, Gordon. Merry Christmas."

"Merry Christmas to you too, Miss Brie." Gordon appeared to be hiding a smile—a broader smile than normal—as he rolled the cart closer to the bed.

She wondered what he was so happy about. Maybe just because it was Christmas.

She was happy about that too.

Cyrus stood waiting while Gordon uncovered the plates and poured the coffee. Then Gordon gave him a strange little nod as he left the room, closing the bedroom door behind him.

"He's all cheery today," Brie said, happily reaching for a cup of coffee.

"Was he?" Cyrus asked, sounding strangely distracted.

Brie frowned at him. "Yes. Didn't you see him? Why are you standing there like that? Come eat breakfast."

Cyrus stepped closer, looking quite adorable in nothing but his red puppy-Santa pajama pants but also a little stiff.

Brie picked up a croissant and noticed that Cyrus was holding something. "What do you have there?" she asked, unable to get a good look at what he held in his hand.

She was starting to take a bite when Cyrus came another step closer to her and lowered himself onto one knee.

She blinked, the croissant poised right at her lips

Cyrus was holding a ring. The most beautiful diamond ring she'd ever seen in her life. It appeared to be an antique. The gold band looked hand engraved with a delicate, intricate scrolling, and the large princess diamond was surrounded by a halo of small rubies.

"Brie Graves," he was saying, gazing up at her with that same adoring look she'd seen in his eyes before. "A year ago, I hadn't thought it possible for me to love you any more than I did then. But every day I love you more. Every day I'm more completely yours. I don't know how I managed to live without you for so long, and I never want to know what it's like to do so again. You're my blessing, my strength, my solace, a gift I'll never deserve. And now I'm asking you to be one more thing to me."

She was frozen, perched on the edge of the bed, still holding the croissant to her mouth.

"Brie Graves," he said, his deep, strong, long-hidden heart naked on his face. "Would you do me the honor of becoming my wife?"

She was washed with waves of surprise, joy, excitement, and tenderness, but she still couldn't seem to move.

Cyrus arched his eyebrows just slightly after the moment stretched on a bit too long. "Just so you know, this position isn't exactly easy on my knees."

She dropped the croissant with a helpless sob and reached down toward him. "Yes," she gasped. "Yes. Oh, yes!"

She was so excited that she almost knocked him over, but he managed to stay upright and maintain his hold on the ring. Then he raised himself up to sit on the bed beside her. He took her left hand and gently slid the ring onto her finger.

She stared down at it, panting audibly, and then she launched herself at Cyrus, pushing him down onto his back on the bed in her excitement.

So they did some more kissing and generally made fools of themselves for a little while until Brie's stomach growled, reminding her that they hadn't eaten breakfast yet.

"Did Gordon know?" Brie asked when they'd finally returned to the tray.

Cyrus chuckled. "Of course he knew. Why do you think he was so excited? He gave me the ring when he brought in the tray. I couldn't leave it in here for fear you'd nose around and find it too soon."

"Sneaky." She shivered giddily as she admired her ring again. She was a little worried about how much the ring must have cost since she was going to be wearing it around everywhere, but it was too beautiful, too special, for her to get too hung up on the price. "I love it."

"Good." Just the one word, but it was clear that her appreciation had meant a lot for him. She wondered just how long and hard he'd searched before he found this incredible ring. Knowing him, he wouldn't have taken anything less than perfect. For her.

She leaned over to kiss his jaw. "I can't believe you surprised me so much. I never expected to get engaged on Christmas morning."

"What more appropriate day could there be for a miracle?" His voice was light, almost dry, but she knew he meant the words sincerely.

She said, "As long as you know you were a miracle to me too."

~

Cyrus was turning off the shower, telling himself that it was really all right for him to feel this giddy, that despite his long history with guilt and responsibility, he was allowed to be this happy, when he heard Brie let out a squeal.

Grabbing a towel to wrap around his hips, he hurried out to see what was wrong, momentarily wondering if it was finally time for payback for all the joy he'd experienced over the past year.

Brie was out on the balcony and had left the door opened.

"Brie," he exclaimed, stepping out to see what she was doing and exhaling with relief when he saw she was all right. "It's freezing out here! You're just wearing your gown."

"It's snowing!" She whirled around, beaming at him, looking rumpled and rosy and happy and like everything he wanted. "It never snows in Savannah."

"Well, it snows here all the time. Now please come in before you get sick."

She gave him an exaggerated frown, but she stepped back into the room and closed the door. "I've never had a white Christmas before."

He felt a little smile play on the corners of his lips. "We can go out and make a snowman later if you want."

She laughed. "You think you're joking, but I'm going to hold you to that, you know."

She probably would.

"If it takes a snowman to make you happy, then a snowman we will make."

Her face was fond and warm, but she said, "Okay, if you don't stop saying sweet things like that, I'm going to have to jump you again. And then we'll be late. Harrison and Marietta will be here soon, you know."

"I know. I promise not to say any more sweet things."

"Just for now. You can say more sweet things later— just so you know."

He twitched his eyebrows. "Understood."

Brie showered while Cyrus got dressed, and then he sat and drank coffee while she rushed through dressing.

He couldn't help but smile when he saw her sneaking looks at her ring every few minutes.

It was just before nine in the morning when they started down the grand staircase. Cyrus reached behind him to take Brie's hand as they descended.

He stopped in surprise when he saw Harrison standing at the bottom, looking up at them, obviously waiting.

"Merry Christmas," he said, taking the final steps down. Brie still clung to his hand.

"Merry Christmas," Harrison said, his eyes searching Cyrus's face. "Is everything good?"

"Of course."

"I mean, with..." Harrison nodded toward Brie instead of finishing the sentence.

Brie laughed and raised her left hand to show him the ring.

Harrison's expression relaxed, and he broke out in a smile. "Oh, thank God. I wanted to make sure, before you went in."

"Before we went in where?" Cyrus asked, completely confused by his nephew's behavior. "Where are Marietta and Melissa?"

"They're in there," Harrison said, nodding toward the closed door of the main living room. "Come say hi."

Cyrus frowned, but he took Brie's hand again and opened the door to the room.

He halted in shock when he discovered that the room was full of people. So many people. Andrew and Laurel. Benjamin and Mandy and Lucy. Jonathan and Sarah and their sons. Mitchell and Deanna. Everyone. Everyone he loved.

Everyone who loved him.

He turned his head in dazed shock to look back at Harrison, who was behind him in the doorway.

Harrison gave a little shrug. "Everyone wanted to be here to celebrate with you. But that's why I had to check first to make sure it all went as planned."

Brie was clinging to his arm. "So everyone knew you were going to ask me this morning?"

"No!" Cyrus stared around at the room filled with smiling faces. "Only Gordon knew."

Gordon was standing near the door, looking as utterly bland as ever. "I may have let it slip to Mr. Harrison, sir. My deepest apologies."

For just a moment the whole world seemed to shudder before his eyes.

Then Cyrus started to laugh.

That was all it took for the room to erupt, and everyone was coming up to hug them, congratulate them, tell them how much they loved them.

Andrew gave Cyrus a bear hug, calling him "Lord Uncle." And Benjamin clapped him on the back and said he got to be the best man. Jonathan was as rumpled and askew as ever as he came over to give his congratulations. He opened his mouth and then closed it, shaking his head and muttering, "Damn. Good job."

Jonathan had never been comfortable expressing feelings, and this was high praise indeed. Cyrus laughed as he gave his nephew a hug.

He glanced over and saw that Brie was practically in tears against her brother's chest.

He turned around to where Harrison was standing next to Marietta. Cyrus tried to say something and couldn't.

"I know," Harrison said before he hugged him. "I feel exactly the same way."

~

The morning was long and rich and full of laughter, and then Gordon and the staff had prepared a lavish dinner that lasted a couple of hours.

So it was late when Cyrus and Brie could finally slip outside alone and enjoy the snow, which had stopped for most of the day but had finally started again.

She told him with a twitching smile that he didn't even have to make her a snowman.

He took her past the Rococo fountain and across the wide lawns to his favorite walled garden, and they walked around, not talking, just holding hands, as the snow fell in gentle flakes on their hats, coats, and hair.

"I'm so happy," she said after a long stretch of deep silence. She glanced down at the beautiful ring on her beautiful hand.

He stopped and turned to face her. "So am I."

Her eyes were full of so many things as she lifted her hands to his shoulders. "You look happy."

"I'm not surprised. I'm too full of happiness to hide it."

"I remember what you looked like last year, when I first saw you staring at our fishing pond painting in Savannah."

"I'm surprised you even noticed me at all."

"Well, I did. Something in you spoke to me. It still does. I want it to always speak to me."

He leaned down to brush his lips against hers. "It always will."

She let out a long sigh. "You looked... like someone I really wanted to know. But you didn't look happy then."

"I wasn't. A lot has happened to me since then."

Her smile was alluring, almost whimsical. "Like what?"

He kissed her again. "Like you."

They walked together in the snow for a long time, and Cyrus watched the walls, the benches, the statuary, the bushes, the trees, the world get covered by a soft, sparkling blanket of white.

It felt like a sign, a symbol, a physical manifestation of his soul, of all he had lived through.

Some sort of quiet benediction.

A promise that the world wasn't just broken. It was also covered by grace.

About Noelle Adams

Noelle handwrote her first romance novel in a spiral-bound notebook when she was twelve, and she hasn't stopped writing since. She has lived in eight different states and currently resides in Virginia, where she writes full time, reads any book she can get her hands on, and offers tribute to a very spoiled cocker spaniel.

She loves travel, art, history, and ice cream. After spending far too many years of her life in graduate school, she has decided to reorient her priorities and focus on writing contemporary romances. For more information, please check out her website: noelle-adams.com.

Books by Noelle Adams

Eden Manor Series
> One Week with her Rival
> One Week with her (Ex) Stepbrother
> One Week with her Husband

Beaufort Brides Series
> Hired Bride
> Substitute Bride
> Accidental Bride

One Night Novellas

One Hot Night: Three Contemporary Romance Novellas

> One Night with her Boss
> One Night with her Roommate
> One Night with the Best Man

Willow Park Series

> Married for Christmas
> A Baby for Easter
> A Family for Christmas
> Reconciled for Easter
> Home for Christmas

Heirs of Damon Series

> Seducing the Enemy
> Playing the Playboy
> Engaging the Boss
> Stripping the Billionaire

Standalones

> A Negotiated Marriage
> Listed
> Bittersweet
> Missing
> Revival
> Holiday Heat
> Salvation
> Excavated
> Overexposed

Road Tripping
Chasing Jane
Fooling Around

The Protectors Series (co-written with Samantha Chase)
Duty Bound
Honor Bound
Forever Bound
Home Bound

Made in the USA
Columbia, SC
04 June 2018